To Terry

May Your Almighty Creator
unveil Your destiny!

Adrushya Guru

A Journey Within

ABC.XYZ

authorHOUSE®

AuthorHouse™
1663 Liberty Drive
Bloomington, IN 47403
www.authorhouse.com
Phone: 1 (800) 839-8640

Published by AuthorHouse 11/27/2017

ISBN: 978-1-5462-0590-6 (sc)
ISBN: 978-1-5462-0589-0 (hc)
ISBN: 978-1-5462-0588-3 (e)

Library of Congress Control Number: 2017913164

Print information available on the last page.

Preface

When I began to write Adrushya Guru, the original plot I had in mind was for it to be crime fiction; it didn't even have this title at that point! However, as the story progressed, Joan – the lead character dragged me towards her inner quest – my Adrushya Guru. As soon as I took that leap of faith into that unknown, the plot course unfolded itself and I became a mere witness and typist of all that was being channeled through me, and the voices I was hearing. I felt torn apart in different aspects and started asking the questions to which I had always wanted the answers.

The vague readings in childhood; arguments with my Muslim friends; the experience of lighting my own father's funeral pyre; a torn old book bought from a junk-dealer; and even my migration to Toronto....... nothing proved to be coincidental; everything was perfectly timed and stacked like book pages in my deep subconscious, only to emerge in the plot.

This all started, may be a few years ago or may be a few births ago, or perhaps it was triggered after reading *The Alchemist* by Paulo Coelho. What a wonderful experience that was for me!! I had just broken up with my first love, with no proper job or even bread in my hands, I was very much in a suicidal state. There was absolutely nothing worth living for in my life. In such depth of despair, one of my Gurus, and friend,

Arpan gave me 'The Alchemist' and it hit me right where it mattered – in the quest for my destiny, right from the first page!

The company of my true friends: Yogi, Daya, Subbu and Santiago not only helped me to stop thinking about ending my life, but also kindled the hope of life beyond where I was. This power of thinking triggered different queries in my mind of: Why do we come into this world? What is the purpose of achieving our destiny? Why should we even have a destiny? What did Santiago do after he got his treasure; did he cease to breathe or did the world collapsed for him? Who was The Alchemist? What is life? What is death?

My curiosity dragged me back to my childhood, when I used to hear the frequent mention of the Journey of Adrushya Guru. My Father, the reason for my meaningful existence in this world, always used to talk about the mysterious Adrushya Guru. This mystery always remained at the back of my mind, waiting for the right time and the right situation to reveal itself. Finally, it reached a boiling point in my life, when I discovered that everything in this mortal world is constrained by time and I have very limited time to explore it. The rest of all my experience is my Adrushya Guru – The Invisible but omnipotent part of me, available for you to discover.

I am sure many of you will find some answers to questions of your own and the journey, itself, as your own. I am as confident as my Adrushya Guru is, that you will have a purposeful experience while delving in this quest of life.

I would like to dedicate this book to my parents *Suman, Surendra Kumar Choubey* – My Real Gurus.

Special regards to my wife *Preeti* and two cute daughters: *Jigmisha* and *Tara*. And, a heartfelt thanks to *Shamanthy, Joyce, Vaibhav, Sanjay* and *Fariha* for their role at various points in this journey of materializing my real dream.

mūlādhāra

(THE CONVERSATION)

--- MVLADHARA ---
(THE CONVERSATION)

An Aghori (who performs occult rituals on dead bodies) priest, clad in a dirty and ripped yellow towel with bare top, disheveled gray beard and long black hair, is reciting a couplet of the famous mediaeval mystic poet; Kabir Das.

"Bura Jo Dekhan Mai Chala,
(When I tried to search for the evil)

Bura Na Milya Koi,
(I met not a single one)

Jo Mai dekhan Aapnu,
(But, when I looked within myself)

Mujhse Bura Na Koi"
(I found no one worse than me)

He pauses to take a large puff of Ganja – traditional marijuana consumed by mendicants to concentrate on their conversations with

God, before explaining the meaning of the phrase he just recited to his audience.

The sound of cracking wood coming from the large fire pit, mixed with the hissing of the wind is deafening at that moment.

"I tried my utter best to find evil in this world, but couldn't find any until..............I looked at myself!" He elaborates. "I find so many qualities in others that can make me even better traveler in the quest of my life; but alas! This one bad quality in me is holding me from exploring my true self, its making me the most horrible person instead. Do you know what that is?" The dozing audiences just shake their head negatively in silence to seek the answer.

"It's lack of open and receptive mind to find evil within instead of in others.

We are always so engrossed in proving ourselves superior to others that we miss the opportunity to rise ourselves towards absolute perfection. We are good wherever we are; it is the sense of being comfortable; and this status-quo hardly matters when it comes to the question of attaining perfection. What matters to us are: our deficiencies, the evil within, and above all, the intention to look at all those ills in order to pull them out from their roots and become even better human; and as we do so, we start inching closer to perfection," he is warming his hands while gauging audience's interest in his explanation.

"Take the example of money; it has no value unless it is used to evaluate something else. We never ever feel that we have sufficient money. Even the richest people in this world persistently work to be wealthier, don't they?" He continues without stopping for an answer from his audience this time. "They understand that, whatever they have is already there. There is no point in boasting about it; they must persevere to work on earning what is not there.

Interestingly, we do not have the same attitude when it comes to working on the good qualities – necessary to make us a better human being. As soon as we find some good within ourselves, we start boasting about it, we start exploiting it. We become arrogant until the good itself diminishes! We hardly try to leverage those qualities to become even better. Rather, we just sit on them and compare with others. We indulge in self-praise instead of self-preening.

Why don't we follow same logic to be good as we do to be wealthy? Ultimately, both provide us to have some form of abundance, don't they? Why don't we follow nature's law to be perfect? Why do we go through the meaningless pain of living and dying; just to get burnt in the fire and disappear from this world?"

Although he is speaking to his audience, his complete focus remains on adjusting the wood in the fire, as if he is speaking to someone in fire pit. Again, he pauses to take a shot at the shared marijuana pot before continuing his lecture.

"We are in a big 'if-then-else' logic. If we decide to do something, we open another loop of 'if-else' logic where success and alternate success lie for us to choose.

Yes, it is 'alternate success'; the one we deserve. Success is what we want. If we succeed, it means we got what we were looking for and we are qualified for it; if not then we get what we deserve. There is nothing called failure. And, this is where we need to start working to be eligible so we deservedly get what we want."

"ADRUSHYA GURU says: This is 'The Law of Return', so start working on what you are destined for in this life. Once you make yourself eligible, the goal automatically falls in place. This whole world and our fate follow The Law of Physics."

He notices an ignorant couple standing in the corner. The girl, an African-American, clad in an Indian sari, is trying to listen to his

3

speech, whereas the man is staring at her and trying to touch her on undesired places.

"Come over here and join us, its cold out there. And don't worry; we Aghoris don't eat live corpses!" The Priest jokes while making some space for the couple. Others in the group, who have already forgotten the topic of discussion, giggle and make space for the couple. Everybody seems to be interested in the woman now.

Both of them take the empty space in the huddle. A dog, tailing the girl sits in front of the girl like an obedient pet.

The Priest resumes his speech. "As you persistently make decisions in your life, nature assesses you for your readiness to move to next level. If you pass, it opens the next path to follow, and if you don't, it presents you with an alternate and longer path to get ready; before the next crossroad arrives. The time to return to the ultimate goal and the path to traverse the distance depends on two things: your commitment to achieve and your eligibility to bear the burden of the achievement.

However, according to my Adrushya Guru, the worst happens when you don't decide; you don't break the stigma; you just remain in a cocoon, dwindling with nature. You look for comfort rather than hardship to rise. This infuriates our Supreme Mother. This attitude results in sudden death, diseases, droughts, and floods and any other way she can show her anger! Because, Mother Nature never remains constant, neither does she want others to be. Every day, every second is a new moment, then why should you be incompatible while repeating stagnated actions and thoughts?"

It has been ages since the girl heard someone speaking English. She had hardly spoken to anybody since she was dumped in this unknown world of predators.

Some of the audiences leave the meeting at first opportunity after sensing the dog's presence. Their swift departure hints at the fear of the unknown within their minds. The strange lust felt due to the presence of a girl at a midnight congregation fire has been overtaken by the even stranger fear of death due to the mere presence of a canine.

The girl is feeling otherwise because of the presence of the Priest. Even in the dark and with her partial blindness, she can appreciate his gaunt face, thanks to the flames oozing out of the fire pit. His amber eyes are intense but distant.

"Welcome to Banaras, Miss! So, what brings you here: A Crime, Commitment or Karma?" Asks the priest while grooming his dirty beard with his hands, he has changed the topic of discussion once again to enquire with an alien black girl. Her appearance is totally out of space and out of time for the city like Banaras. Her pet, a husky dog with two color eyes is adding to the confusion here. The dog is howling like a wolf while looking at the strange bonfires on the bank of the river Ganges.

"Her name is B-Cube. I am sure you would've heard about her," boastingly interrupts the man with the girl. Even in the farthest of comparisons, this companion does not look anything like a tourist friend of the girl. They are in *the business* instead.

A (beautiful) black American girl dressed like an Indian woman, coupled with an average (looking) Indian boy who is more interested in her body than a relationship. A strange dog who is more interested in protecting the girl, sitting around the huge fire pit at the famous bank of river Ganges in Banaras, India – a city ancient to history – the center of universe as per Indian mythology, listening to an Aghori – the companion of the dead. What a sight to behold!

Every person in the circle peaks around in amazement to have a closer look at the strange and mystical woman with a familiar name.

The companion counters the Priest sarcastically. "Who are you to ask such questions? Are you a police officer? Is this the way you speak to your guests?"

"You have the eyesight no one else has; your ears can 'see' the things that no one can hear," the Priest talks straight to the girl while ignoring her companion. His cryptic language explains the fact that the girl is partially blind but well trained to use her hearing power to judge what lies ahead.

Priest's eyes are red as if he hadn't slept for ages. His yellowish teeth are shining in the flames as those try to reach the sky.

The fire pit at the center is unusually big to keep few people warm. There are other similar fires burning around this congregation, but with no one around. It's also a bit smelling like flash burning in it. A very strange backdrop is prevailing in the middle of the night on the riverbank of Ganga.

The dog continues to howl until the Priest rises from his seat and pulls a peculiar red-hot bowl-shaped object out of the flames, dips it into the water stream and then puts the steaming white object in front of the dog. The strange object is actually broken top of human skull and the big fire pit is nothing but a funeral pyre! The riverbank is nothing but the famous cremation ground of Banaras!

The dog gets busy with the skull. Her tongue is licking the warm salty ashes on the skull. The vapor emanating from the eyeholes is resulting in an enigmatic sight. The playful dog and her game are enough to frighten some more audiences.

"Who was behind those eyes?"

"What was the purpose of his or her life?"

"Was he or she here just to be burnt one day, so that a strange dog can come and lick his or her skull? Is this all we yearn for in our lives?" These are some of the questions storming in almost everybody's mind as they sit around the pyre intensely watching the dog.

The Priest understands the curiosity in his audience's mind. "Should you let your Adrushya Guru ask questions? Do not stop him or yourself, don't be afraid of him. He asks questions before he starts answering them. Adrushya Guru must know that you do not have answers to everything, and then only is he going to answer for you.

He is right there in front of you, because, all of you have been at that miraculous moment when nothing else mattered. That moment was nothing but your birth, when Adrushya Guru inspired you to open your eyes and breathe air."

He pauses to pour some honey on top of the skull. The honey spreads all over the skull and mixes with the ash stuck to the skull.

The sweetness of honey lures the dog to lick the warm skull even more rigorously. The audience can clearly hear the slurps of dog. Their expressions change as the taste of the ash. The priest laughs at this sudden change in perception of his audience.

"We all think like a beast. Look at yourselves; earlier you were thinking about the morbidity of being mortal, and then turning into ashes, but now, we are more curious that how it tastes to have honey mixed with human ash!

This is where we actually convert from psyche to materialism.

Your Adrushya Guru appeared in front of you, made all of you blank when you faced the only inevitable fact of this world – Truth of Death. If you start living with this fact, it will let you live to the fullest, but if you try to run away from it, thinking you can get away, it will catch you at its own time. Death is nothing but the only truth in this world. Subsequently, he dragged you back in to materialism by playing with my and the dog's mind: How is the honey, is it sweet? How does it taste with salt? You have been slung from the moment of truth to another world of taste at the blink of an eye."

"You need to cross roads carefully mister," he again abruptly stops his discussion to address the girl's companion.

"Haha, you Aghori, just pray and smoke, that's what suites you cannibals; chant the mantras but please don't speak philosophy. You people living with the dead cannot teach living beings about the life," the person laughs off his own statement while fearfully avoiding the straight glare from the Priest.

"Vinash Kale Vipareet Buddhi," now the Priest responds with a phrase in Sanskrit.

"What does that mean?" The black girl breaks the silence and drags people's attention away from the approaching procession.

"That means nothing! This Aghori is a gone case," interrupts the man hurriedly.

A long silence settles amongst the audience. A funeral procession is approaching from the distance led by monotonous drumbeats played by half-asleep musicians. This is first funeral gathering of the day, but some of the pyres from the previous day are still active.

Some caretakers on the ground get busy in pulling out half-burnt human bodies from the pyres and dragging them down to the Ganga, while others get busy in scavenging the half-charred wood from those fires. They are careful to not to touch the bones though. An indistinct boatman in the distance is trying to pull these bodies out of the water and piling them into his vessel.

"Since I have the eligible audience today, I am going to move away from tonight's discussion of The Law of Return to 'The Power of Commitment to the Truth' in this world.

When you have truth with you; your death stands right beside you as a friend, instead of sitting on your head as an enemy.

Women are a supreme power in this world. They have given birth to each and every mortal creature on this earth. I think it must be a woman who has given birth to this universe."

Most of the people are already feeling bored by now but they can still connect mention of birth with sex and stare at the girl to fantasize about their role in an imaginary conceiving process. There is a clear distinction between topic of discussion and perception of audience.

"It's not sex that brings life to a living being, but rather, that ultimate moment within the womb of the mother, when the thought is seeded, and it is this very thought that follows the creation of the new world into the mind of a baby.

Remember! This world is nothing but a thought standing on the foundation of truth; without thought there is nothing: light or the absence of light; day-night; all are nothing but our thoughts."

By now, only the girl amongst the audience is listening to him, the others are more interested in peeking inside her disheveled blouse. Their attention is stuck in the ultimate illusion of their life: Sex.

The fear of death, the chill of the wind, the bitterness of the truth; all are overshadowed by the tides of imagination of having sex with one of the most talked about women in town.

The Priest keeps smoking and passing the pot to the others in the huddle. Even the girl is part of the community smoking now.

"Adrushya Guru says that the trigger of thought is not spontaneous, it's inspired by the thoughts of the mother," he pauses to look at a freshly lit funeral pyre burning at the distance. "This stimulation of thought has been carried over and enhanced by mothers for millions of years."

These words of praise for the mother mesmerize the girl. Perhaps it is very first time that she is hearing some good words about motherhood; until now she has experienced only womanhood and its lust.

"And this transition is one of the reasons why a mother is so sensitive, so pure and so nice; because, these characteristics need to be passed from her to the next generation in a better form at a much more evolved stage. She is the one carrying our progression in her thoughts."

"But wait!" The Priest's expression changes from a smiling rebuttal to an ironic grin.

"Do you see Mother Ganga here?" The Priest asks while pointing to the river stream.

"She has been flowing with the same passion for millions of years."

"She is the purest of all the water streams; she has her way defined even when she emerges out of the Himalayas as a tiny water stream trickling out of the glaciers.

Sometimes she is violent and on other occasions she is calm, but, that's because her goal is not to reach the ocean and become part of a single big pond, no," he pauses to fix the wood in the fire pit. Now he is looking into the eyes of the girl and speaking only to her. "Now you might be thinking: then what's her goal? The purpose of her eternal flow is to serve people, destroy who comes in her way and her objective, without any prejudice and to benefit the ones who are neediest.

You do what you are destined to do without bringing any sense of defeat, ego, pride and sorrow in your mind. Flow like river Ganga and even when you are in the ocean, you will maintain your identity until your goal is achieved," his eyes are closed and looking at the infinite within.

"Maa Ganga is your guide now, because she knows that your and her destiny is same. She knows that she is not flowing in this world for any other reason than to serve. And this service is called: The Law of Return.

Go and merge in the ocean, you will realize your goal when it's the right time," he again pauses in the middle of his statement. It is three o'clock in the morning! The man accompanying the girl wakes up with a jerk, pulls out a gun out of nowhere and points it at the Priest, he is scared, and perhaps he had a nightmare.

"Now, his ego is hurt that he has wasted all of his time here instead of taking you somewhere to have sex," the Priest tells the girl without any fear on his face.

The girl gently puts one of her hands on the man's private part, just below his belly. His defense is down by the mere touch of the girl. She takes the gun and moves away from the congregation followed by the man and the dog. The couple with the dog is pacing up the steep steps.

The Priest stands up to look at them; the stream of funeral processions has picked up pace now, with a continuous influx of the dead carried by their relatives.

The boatman has become even busier in collecting the charred bodies.

"And, this act was not at all egoist so there is no wrong in this!" The Priest shouts at girl from behind.

ṣvadhishthana

(THE LIBERATION)

--- SVADHISHTHANA ---
(THE LIBERATION)

The male companion of the girl dies in a freak accident shortly afterwards. He apparently slips in front of a moving truck while crossing the road.

A shadow is following them from a distance. The follower is aware of the fact that the girl herself actually pushed the man under the truck intentionally. To her rescue, she has perfect excuse that the man was drunk as well as high on marijuana. The girl and her dog are saved only by their fate.

The shadow continues to follow until the girl reaches an otherwise prohibited area. It is the red-light district of the holy city. The girl is none other than part of the world's oldest trading system.

--- ◆ ◆ ◆ ◆ ---

Back in the brothel, the girl has become notorious, not for being a foreign black girl, but for the risk, she carries for her clients.

Quite often playing with fire becomes a fantasy for miss-adventurists. Girl's notoriety has become a wildfire in town. More and more audacious people are turning to the brothel to try their luck. It is a different story though, that almost everyone who comes there boasting, stops only at certain point, where he just demonstrates his superiority by sexually assaulting the girl and satisfying his ego. They leave the house with cooked up stories that they have taken infamous B-Cube on a ride to the city and remained alive to tell such fables. Some do try and never return to talk about their experiences with the girl.

Girl is happy because not only she is earning money but also her disgusting desire to keep the pain of sexual assaults is alive. Why would she want to have such painful and humiliating rewards for herself?

Its autumn descending on the city now with frostier nights and foggy mornings, the Priest visits the brothel in his typical attire, it is a highly unusual visit to the brothels. No celibate person has ventured on these streets since Vatsyayana visited them to write the epic Kamasutra. The Priest adores Tripund, which is a three-liner mark on his forehead and white ash on his body. He talks to the headmistress who is sitting in his feet with her head down due to respect as well as fear to Aghoris. His loud voice instils cold-water shivers in the girl's heart. She feels the same positive vibes that she experienced at the Ganga's riverbank. Somewhere inside, she is feeling that her departure from this hell on earth is very near.

She hears a lot of giggles and laughter from downstairs. Some prostitutes are mocking the Priest that he has befallen to the sin of falling in love with a whore.

"Get ready to kill another egomaniac cannibal male chauvinist and make this world a bit of a better place," the messenger delivers an abusive but hopeful command to the girl. Abusive, because other girls in the brothel are jealous of the American girl's fame and ridiculous demand; at the same time hopeful, because they think she will kill all the sexomaniac rapists whose egos are stiffer than their private parts.

"I will pray that he doesn't eat you alive!" She leaves girl in the middle of confusion with this final warning.

Finally, amongst the laughter, bantering and curses, she leaves with the Priest. Headmistress is furious and all the respect in a sadhu is gone, but fear of an Aghori's wrath is holding her from retaliating. They look like a bizarre couple walking on the streets of Banaras – an eccentric prostitute with an ascetic Aghori. They don't look like a couple, nor do they look like close relatives.

The Priest tries to lead the walk but the girl is fast enough to catch his steps whenever she is left behind. It may be true that their business is different, but it appears that they are equal on their quest to their ultimate goal.

"You were talking about 'The Law of Return' the other day," girl breaks the long silence between them. "Can you explain what this law is?"

"What are you looking for," asks the Priest.

"I don't know."

"Then how do you expect to get an answer?"

"Well, it is too early for me to say or even think what I am looking for," she pauses for a moment to look at the serenity of the river stream amidst the rising silence of the setting sun.

"Nothing is early or late in this realism. Everything is timed perfectly," the Priest interrupts her admiration of river Ganga.

"It is us, the fools, who try to adjust our ego by connecting it with the three swords of time: Birth, Life and Death, and say what is early or late or on time."

"Coming back to your question about the Law of Return; Adrushya

Guru says: it is the law of gravity, the law of momentum of inertia, or even the law of energy which you might be aware of."

"Wait, who is Adrushya Guru?" The girl interrupts. "I heard this mysterious phrase from you a couple of times the other night."

The Priest continues to elaborate on her first query without paying attention to the girl's deviation from the original question. "In very simple terms, if you put effort into your goal, you will achieve it, but the success factor or the efficiency of your psychic motor to attain the goal depends on the commitment you put into it.

If you give your fullest to nature, nature will return the favor accordingly.

If you give with good intention, you get good in return, if you do bad so shall you reap it. It is such a simple thing, yet one of the toughest for this smart world to understand.

When a mother decides to become a Kaali, it shows how much energy she holds. She becomes the ultimate symbol of destruction. Even a supreme commander of this world cannot stop her from bringing an apocalypse to the world."

"Now who is this mother Kaali, is she the Adrushya Guru? What is her story? Why are you confusing me with so many mysterious names?"

The Priest is still in his own flow of conversation. "Violence is a natural process, necessary to weed out the extremities from the world. Actually, if you do not have anger, you cannot have fire in you. However, one has to be cautious that this anger be pure. It must not connect with materialistic goals, and it must not be the means of satisfying your ego – never.

Then the question arises: why do we have ego? Moreover, how is it possible to detach anger from ego? It is almost impossible but still: almost; there must be a reason to bring forth our anger, and this reason must be pure and selfless.

Killing someone just because he has hurt you is not a reason, because you are never truly hurt. Your soul is invincible, but it is your ego, that is as fragile as glass; it looks beautiful when people admire it, but when time tests it, it breaks.

Regarding Kaali's story, she was a Hindu Goddess who ran havoc on this world, not because the messengers of the God killed her father, but because, God itself had crossed the line of being good. The Godheads should have exercised their duty of being forgiving instead of exercising their right to avenge selfishly. This eliminated the fine line between Gods and Demons. Had Kaali not taken this violent path to teach God about its duty, this world would have been different today."

"Interesting," murmurs the girl attentively...

"Interesting, indeed! Jesus sacrificed his life for his belief because he was sure that picking a sword to defend the undefeatable would only add to humiliation of his God. It was not God itself who was bringing this unto him; it was not that he hadn't built a solid foundation to convey God's message," the Priest further explains.

"But if that's the case then why did Kaali do this," the girl asks.

"Because it was her destiny, she was born to do this. She had her goal clearly defined and that was to be a companion to the Supreme of the beings itself, and this doesn't fit into Kaali's own philosophy. And that's what ensued thereafter; the Supreme Being realized its mistake and corrected itself."

"Why are you calling Supreme God – It?" The girl counters the priest.

"Do you have any literary addressing for God's gender?" the Priest responds calmly,

"It, God is an experience not a tangible physical object, and it is such an experience!"

"Alright, English and Grammar aside, so what should I do?"

The Priest is already in an apparition; staring deep in the sky with no control over his eyeballs or other body parts.

--- MANIPURA ---
(THE FIRE OF WISDOM)

The Priest, accompanied by the girl keeps wandering in the narrow gullies of the Banaras. His condition is that of a mad man, who hardly knows his destination. Finally, he stops in front of the door of a thatched hut. It is a ramshackle house made of bare walls with roof of straws; it does not even have a door lock. There are many cryptic red marks around the door and on the walls of the hut. Perhaps, these marks are enough to deter the thieves from breaking in. He struggles to open the jammed door; just like the girl's heart struggles to let her go inside the hut; it is afraid that it might be trapped in this cannibal psycho's den forever.

The pungent smell of marijuana and incense sticks and just one oil lamp burning inside as source of light, adds to her doubts. The girl is scared, but still entering, doubtful yet following; uncertain, but still venturing inside those dark walls.

Priest offers her a small wooden plank to sit. Most of the room is barely visible except an exhaustive prayer altar due to fade light. The girl, being partially blind does not need lights to understand what is going on.

Although she is preparing herself to deal with any eventualities, still she is a bit more afraid than usual. She is missing something very important in her defense but not able to figure out what that thing is. The Priest, still in the realm of his illusive world, lights two more oil lamps. Now the room is a bit bright, still not bright enough for the girl to look at things properly.

"Will you be my Kaali today?" He whispers in the girl's ear.

"Are you Shiva?" Responds the girl, anticipating the Priest is just trying to fantasize a dirty game. Her agreeable response comes with the hope that it may surprise the Priest and prolong the unknown so that she can overcome the night.

"No mother, I am not Shiva, I am your son: I am Aghori!" The Priest responds with a sobbing voice with tears rolling down and disappearing in his thick beard.

"Well, as long as you don't kill me, I am your property for tonight. So yes, if you wish, I am your Kaali."

"Maa, Ohh Mother, my dearest mother!" The Priest cries with joy and falls down at the girl's lap. She is sitting with her legs crossed and her back leaning against a patchy mud-wall.

"You are the one who can kill even death, time and space," he says as he kisses her feet.

"Please accept my offerings," the Priest offers her a bowl with some liquid.

The girl is mesmerized and surprised by how the situation is unfolding. She suddenly starts feeling thirsty, takes the bowl and gulps it. She vomits it out as fast as she has drunk it. It is a very bitter and strange liquid; she knows how beer and wine and even whisky tastes but this is something different. In fact, this is not even Indian made country liquor that she was forced to drink many times at the brothel.

"Is it a poison or some strange sedative?" Her brain is trying to think of the worst possible experience it may have encountered. However, it is too late for her to react; some of the liquid has already gone down her throat and showing effect.

Although she is gradually losing control over her physical body, her vision is becoming clearer with complete awareness of her surroundings. She is now sitting and watching what is going on without any control over her body. Her hands are frozen; her legs feel like they are strapped to the ground. She cannot even blink.

Her heart is pounding with fear but she has no choice. Only one thing is comforting her now: that she is not going to die blind today. She will experience what is going to happen to her.

Now, she is curious to know whether things can go any worse than her cruel past. She is staring at the Priest, who is decorating a prayer altar around her. She has become the center of his prayers now. The Priest has some garlands, incense sticks, an oil lamp and some colors in a silver plate. She can even see the liquid in the bowl she has just drunk. She has just consumed blood! The thought of drinking blood is enough for her to throw up her stomach, but she cannot, her complete body is simply immobile.

She is recalling all the events that have unfolded in last few days since she met this Priest on the bank of the Ganga. It was a familiar trap laid down around her to become game for a psychopath.

The Priest is sitting in front of her with tears still rolling out of his swollen eyes.

He slowly pours a pail of water over her head. She is completely drenched. She wants to shiver but to no avail; she is like a stone but with senses.

The Priest slowly drapes her in a red sari above her wet clothes. After covering her with dry clothes, he applies a red color on her forehead. He sits in front of her and puts a garland around her neck. He takes out another garland-like object from a closed basket and wraps it around her neck. This black garland is crawling, she can feel the sensation of a slithering animal on her chest but she cannot see it. It is actually a snake! She finds out as soon as it raises its head in front of her eyes. She has a black cobra, nothing short of two meters in length, coiled around her neck and shoulders and staring at her with anger.

The cobra is tightening its coil around her neck and in no mood to get down; the rush of blood in the girl's veins is about to explode; she wants to run away from this place as soon as possible but, she is helpless.

Amidst the loud chanting by the Priest, she recalls this very same psycho's statement that when things seem to be out of control, become water – let yourself float in water. If you know how to remain calm, water will take you to the bank, but if you start struggling with it, it will drown you in its depth.

Slowly, she comes face-to-face with the reality that certain times in our life are like roller coaster rides; one can enjoy oneself, scream the hell out, or simply pass off while being tossed around by the rails, you can laugh or cry, it doesn't matter to the present. Now, when she is feeling freezing cold in wet clothes; and a venomous snake is coiled around her neck, she decides to enjoy the moment. Her eyes are fixed on the sweets placed right in front of her. Truly, we think like beasts. She starts feeling hunger pangs and her attention switches from facing death to feeding herself, its wonderful thing called life!

She assumes that the snake is not going to bite her, because she is not even aware if she is breathing, let alone whether the snake considers her a threat.

The Priest lights a few more oil lamps around her, and now that she is a bit settled with her enemy – her fear; these lamps are enough for her to feel some warmth in her shivering body.

She is looking at the Priest, who has just finished his chanting and is slowly moving towards her. Heart at its best again; as soon as it senses some trouble, it starts pumping but without any success to cause a reaction in her body.

The Priest comes closer, gently opens her mouth by pressing on her chin and feeds her a piece of sweet. The most wonderful thing is occurring to her now! She got what she wanted but she did not seek what she needed – her body control.

She has a piece of sweet cake in her mouth but she is so petrified that she cannot even taste it. It feels like something is melting and dripping inside her throat but no sensation, no taste in her tongue!

The Priest again bows in front of her and then goes back to his seat. Now he lights a fire in a small clay fire pit. While it starts to kindle, the Priest, still chanting his mantras, takes out a sword and comes right towards her. She is afraid again, but not nervous anymore, she knows that she has just learnt to float. It is only a matter of time to keep calm or struggle with herself; because, everything else is immaterial.

The Priest cuts his own right-hand thumb with the sword and blood spews out of it.

He applies this blood onto the girl's forehead, with drops trickling down her face.

"The fire is ready, now what is next," is the thought floating in her mind while she is busy in weaving different combinations of how she can be killed and comparing those against her only one option to live – and that is to just live; one moment at a time.

She is with a stranger who is a psycho, she cannot move. She has a snake around her neck. She is completely wet on a cold night of November. She has drunk what seems to be poisoned blood; leaving her paralyzed. She has a fire burning in front of her, and, she doesn't even have control over her body to protect herself if she falls on her face right in the fire.

She decides to do just one thing – To Live.

Live, whatever time she may have left with herself: a minute, an hour, a painful night or a morning with the flu and cold or even the next turning point to move towards her ultimate goal, one that she had almost forgotten in last few hours. This very thought of achieving her goal brings chilling sensation in her spine. What is this goal? What is she looking for?

◆ ◆ ◆ ◆ ◆ ◆

"That's right! Just do it and see for yourself, what wonders we can experience during the most testing times in our life!" She is amazed at hearing her own voice. She can clearly see herself standing right behind the fire pit, dressed strangely with a skull in her one hand and a heavy dagger in the other.

"Whatever happens, it happens for our good, provided we look at the brighter side of it. If we keep on looking to find the bad, we will get only bad. This is the Law of Return," her alter image is instructing her.

A small turbulence occurs in the fire pit as the Priest throws some powder in it and the deity-self of the girl disappears.

Her eyes start to close slowly, she does not realize that she is feeling the sweetness in her mouth and she is trying to chew the sweet in it. She has warmth on her skin and tiredness on her eyelids that are slowly shutting down.

Her ears are still hearing Aghori's loud hymns coming from a distance that is tending to be infinite.

The girl wakes up to the noise of some kids playing outside. Their noise reminds her of the chorus of early morning birds, playing and singing in the deep woods of Pennsylvania, USA; her birthplace. She finds the Priest busy making tea while reading newspaper. She has a clear view of the hut now. It is nothing but a one-room cottage with a kitchen, bedroom and hall all combined; a perfect example of the bare minimum required in a person's life. It is a squeezed but serene accommodation for one person.

Her wet clothes are lying on one side with one white sari casually wrapped around her. The Priest serves her bed tea and goes to pray in the other corner of the room. The strong smell emanating from burning incense sticks is filling the room fast again. The girl gets ready to go back to her house when the Priest interrupts her, "I know you can't see properly." The girl is amazed and shocked at his revelation. It is the first time that someone has caught her pretending to have perfectly normal vision.

"Moreover, you forgot the dog, so it will be nearly impossible to walk on the close gullies of Banaras."

The girl is even more amazed. "How in this sane world it is possible for me to leave the most honest and reliable companion, who is closer than my own skin to me." It is first time in her life she has left BREACH, her dog and walked out of her room, let alone the house.

"Was I in so much lust to have sex with this person? Was I simply too selfish to go home so I forgot the only one who kept me alive during all these challenges of life?" A storm of questions is raging in her brain again. It is our mind that gets scared so quickly and starts planting negative thoughts, going downwards is so easy for all of us.

The girl, who felt momentary peace after years, gets violent again!

It seems to be a bit of deliberate attempt to be angry by an otherwise suppressed girl. She picks up her bag, takes out a wooden pestle and tries to penetrate it into her private part, right in front of the Priest. This behavior of hers is bizarre! She is deliberately trying to hurt herself and in a place where it may hurt her even more throughout the whole day.

The Priest stops her from doing so and puts the pestle back in her bag.

"What is this all about? Why do you want to give yourself pain and that too in an area of your body which is the origin of this world?"

"Because I don't want to be at peace, I am Kaali! And won't rest until I achieve what I am destined to."

"But how will this anger keep your passion ignited and for how long," the Priest asks.

"I don't know. And I don't want to know either," the girl responds. "What I do know is: this is the only way I can keep my anger alive right now. When future will be realized as present, I will take it the way it will occur."

The Priest laughs while reciting a poem.

"Adrushya ke Andhakaar mai tu Gyan ko Tatolataa hai
Bhavishya ke aadhaar par tu vartmaan ko taulta hai
Krodh na kar, ki jigyasa tujhe manzil par lejayegi
Pidha jitni chahe le-le, qayamat waqt se pale na ayegi
Drudh Nischay, drudh sankalp, bechain man, hathi buddhi
Bas nikal ja, kuud ja pahaad se pagal, sone se nahi
Aankho mai tuffan bharne se hi manzil ayegi!!"
(One cannot find knowledge in the darkness of the unknown,
One cannot define his present solely based on the expected future,
It is not anger but curiosity, which is the key to success

No matter how much one suffers, death is inevitable at its own time.
Become determined and stubborn,
Ignite your heart and go all out to war; don't sleep,
don't rest unless you achieve your goal!)

"Adrushya Guru says: there is always a way to achieve one's goal, but the first thing is to know what the goal is."

"Which country is this?" The girl changes the subject because she does not want to tell her dark past to a stranger, even though the Priest appears to be a genuine psychotic person.

"Don't you know? For how long have you been living in that hell?" the surprised Priest asks her, but continues without waiting for a reply.

"This is India, the land of pantheons, the interpreter of a hole as Zero; to the land of the people, who are so much more obsessed with the hole rather than the Zero."

"What??" the girl's mind has gone blank; she has no idea of how she landed in India, or what she is doing here. She had heard about this country of snake charmers but never encountered an Indian before.

'What is going on? How am I going to find him?' It was hardly a minute since the storm of questions had left her brain; and yet here is another, bigger and stronger than the earlier one.

Her expressions are clearly indicative of a mysterious story behind her. She is lost in thoughts. It is obvious that all the stories and inspirational conversations she has been listening about achieving goals were mere stories. There is no definitive practical logic behind them. They are just a few words to bring peace or solace to the dying or to the depressed so that they can count their days more easily.

The girl gets up from the bed and puts on her wet clothes. She is oblivious to the fact that Priest, who was calling her mother last night, is standing right in front of her.

"Are you going to drop me back to my place?" She asks while trying to figure out the way to drape herself in a sari.

"No, you don't have to go to that place anymore. You are out of that hell," says the Priest

"What do you mean?"

"In very plain words, I bought you for two hundred thousand rupees," answers the Priest coldly.

"How much is that in dollars?"

"Around four thousand US dollars," is the reply from the Priest. "But what does that matter?"

"I heard many times that I am being paid in rupees by my rapists but never realized it is in India that I am working as a whore."

"Did you like it?" The Priest asks.

"Well, its relative, the more they raped me the more painful it was, but on the other hand it made me even more determined to attain the goal of my life," the girl says by sagging down on the bed; she is still half naked. "But, looks like my pain was not enough; and my commitment not a hundred percent. I think I am not yet ready and perhaps never will be to become a real Kaali in this world," she continues with tears rolling down her cheeks.

"How old are you?" the Priest furthers the conversation.

"I don't know. I never counted the days since I landed in this place! Even before that, perhaps." The girl replies in a sudden hurry to get ready to find her only friend, Breach.

"I think I still need to go back," she says with urgency.

"Why?" The Priest is still sitting in a towel and doesn't look like he's in a hurry.

"I need to find Breach."

"Ha-ha," laughs the Priest. "Breach from your fear or from your goal or from your life?"

"I mean I need to get Breach – my dog back!"

"Oh!! No worries, the 'Breach' is right here outside of the house. That's why kids are making so much noise, looks like she also likes their company," he calms the girl down.

"What?" She rushes out but falls down after banging her head on the door.

The Priest helps her stand up; she has a minor cut on her forehead with blood trickling out of it. He wipes the blood off and let's Breach come inside by opening the broken door. Breach has been waiting to join the girl. She straightaway lunges on her and starts to lick her fresh wound with excitement. The girl has forgotten everything in this world now.

Who says nothing can travel faster than light? Our mind certainly does this all the time. It is such a flickering wonder; it takes just a moment for it to move from one level to a whole new one.

"You may get infected with rabies," the Priest cautions the girl.

"Doesn't matter.…..doesn't matter if I die like a dog or as a human being! In fact, I would prefer to die like a dog instead," the girl is clearly expressing her grudge against humanity.

"I still have some money preserved in that house."

"That money was part of the deal," the Priest explains.

"Ok, what next? Can you help me to get to the US embassy please?"

"Are you from America? There is no US embassy here, and beyond that, I think the real question is: do you truly want to leave your journey in the middle to go back from where you started?" The Priest counters her, as he gets ready to go out.

"Oye Pundit!" An unknown but warm and friendly shout from

the outside diverts their attention from the seemingly argumentative discussion.

"Come in BHAIJAN," the Priest responds.

An apparently devout Muslim enters the room with a bag. Bhaijan is the same person who was collecting the half-burnt bodies from the riverbank the other day. The smell emanating from his bag indicates that there is some fresh and warm food in it.

Bhaijan is beyond shocked to see a black alien, especially a female black alien, in the room of one of the most devout Hindu priests in town. The girl's dress is also not telling the exact story of what happened the night before; and the half-naked Priest is further adding to the confusion. Bhaijan is trying to figure out what the story may be.

He does not know the fact that the girl is partially blind, which is the case with most people in town who have met the girl on different occasions. Adding further to Bhaijan's shock, he also finds a dog in the bed!

"How many bodies today?" enquires the indifferent Priest to Bhaijan, who has disgusting confusion showing on his face.

A blazing flash of light passes through the girl's memory. She is afraid once again! Her mind is ready to retaliate if a psycho, a new common species among humans, is attempting to trap her.

"Got thirty since morning today, there was an accident in the nearby town so there were twenty bodies more than the daily average, and we haven't even passed the noon. Some of them are not even half burnt, so we better start early," Bhaijan replies.

The girl has become even more suspicious; she is not able to understand the context even though conversation is in perfect English.

All of her assumptions are now making sense to her: a deeply troubled psychotic priest, who wants to befriend his prey to play with their emotions before giving them a horrific death. But, *that* is not what

30

she is destined for in her life. She is ready to fight it out till the end. She can deal with two average people, especially when she has Breach with her as well. But to the girl's wonder, Breach is not reacting! Is the dog not sensing the same impending danger that she is? What has happened to her? Has she been fed with sedatives, or has this psycho taken control of her emotions as well?

Bhaijan easily catches the girl's attacking gestures and abhorrence of being in yet another mess of hunters and prey.

"Don't worry about us; I am as shocked to see a girl in this place as you are to see two insane people talking about half burnt dead bodies. So calm down and let the Pundit: The Priest explains this," Bhaijan assures her to mitigate her fear.

"She thinks we are psychos not just insane, Bhaijan," the Priest jokes with him.

"Well, yeah, that's something I can explain to you; at least my version," the girl becomes a bit relaxed as she tries to defend her opinion about them.

"I am the infamous whore B-Cube of Banaras," the girl introduces herself.

This introduction is enough for Bhaijan to sag into the only chair in the room.

"Pundit! I can't believe you would go this far in your quest to find your goal of life. It is not right brother; it is dojakh – hell that this behavior will take you to. How can you deviate from your path? Is this the new way to achieve the goal of your life?" Bhaijan angrily scolds the Priest.

The composed Priest wants to say something but the girl interrupts him.

"Let me finish first," she interjects. "He hasn't even touched me inappropriately since I have been here, in fact he bought me for four thousand dollars," she continues while looking at the Priest who is buttoning up his long saffron shirt. "And for what reason, only he knows."

"Pundit, may I ask what's going on here? What is this bitch doing in this holiest of the temples in the holiest of the cities I know of?" Bhaijan is not ready to calm down.

Both the girl and Bhaijan are looking at the Priest now. Breach is licking Priest's feet.

"I don't know," is the simple answer without any reaction from the Priest.

"Then who the hell knows, your Adrushya Guru?" The Girl and Bhaijan retort simultaneously.

"I saw her on the bank and then felt a cool breeze from the Ganga that touched me deep inside my soul, carrying with it her voice, pain and commitment to achieve her goal. I just thought of doing what my Adrushya Guru told me to do," the Priest explains from the depth of his heart and soul, which removes all the mystery from the situation, the truth is straight and it goes deep inside our heart.

"You and your Adrushya Guru, one day both of you are going to jump into Ganga Maa," Bhaijan is still not convinced, but sarcastically laughs off the justification.

The Priest also laughs it off and picks up his torn bag stuffed with papers and other things. He is ready to head out.

"May I ask once again, what is Adrushya Guru?" Enquires the girl once again, as she follows the Priest.

"Nothing," replies the Priest.

"It is everything to this Aghori. Some invisible power, as they say in Sanskrit: Adrushya means: Invisible, Guru: Great – a great invisible guiding force," counters Bhaijan.

"It is Allah for me, Shiva for him, Jesus for Christians and other names for anyone else who wishes to define or personalize their deity."

"Wow! I don't believe in religion or faith or in God anymore," comes as an ice-cold response from the girl. "And here I am, standing and existing as much as you guys with your Adrushya Guru or so called – God."

"No, then it's you, yourself, who is your Adrushya Guru – the invisible force that guides you to be specific. It has nothing to do with only God. Actually, we have two aspects of ourselves: one is within and the other is rest of the world. Once you travel from outside to this inwardly dimension of yours, you find your Adrushya Guru," Bhaijan tries to defend the unknown.

The Priest smiles as the group leave the narrow lanes of Banaras.

With Breach leading their way, they enter a place called *Manikarnika Ghaat* at the riverbank of the Ganges. This place is crammed with old temples. Every building here is an adobe of the God, even if it is completely dilapidated, you will find a God living in it. Bells are ringing all around. A newlywed couple is getting a photo-shoot done with funeral pyres burning as the backdrop.

"What's this pungent barbecue-like smell here? Also, I can't figure out whether people are laughing or crying in those groups around the fire pits," the girl asks out of the curiosity.

"That's the world's busiest funeral home – the heaven-port. People, who are not sure they did any good work during their lives, come to Banaras, so that they can die in the very first city created by God. Once they are dead, this is the departure point for their mortal bodies to be immersed in water and their souls to catapult into the sky. They merge and become one with Earth, Water, Sky, Fire and Air – the five basic elements of the universe," the Priest explains.

"I've heard people mourn boundlessly when someone dies in India! So, what's the laughter all about," the girl wonders.

"That is life. It persists and remains optimistic: giggling, smiling, crying, angry, sad and even happy when someone is embarking on the other journey," the Priest explains further.

"And this is the confluence of all the emotions; a place of spiritual pasteurization.

You tourists, you remain incomplete in your quest to visit India when you come to see the Taajmahal only. Come here to Banaras and look at the beauties of life.

A dying, a dead and a deadly!" He points to lord Shiva's tall statue as he utters his last word.

The girl is able to see things clearly due to bright sunlight. She has never seen cremation of a dead body earlier in her life. She is feeling mesmerized by the mere sense of being so close to death.

"This is the Law of Return. This is what the Holy Gita and the Bible and the Quran try to teach us, but people find themselves stuck in the 'how-to-do' instead of the 'what-to-do' or the 'why-do-to'.

If you really know 'why' to do 'what', then the 'how' is just a matter of time to understand. One attempt or another, failure after failure, we get it one day, provided we know what to achieve.

Imagine you are thinking about 'how' to eat, even before knowing 'what' to eat. Does it sound logical?" the Priest questions the girl.

"No, of course not, what if I am thinking about 'how' to eat a sandwich but only soup is served? It is stupid to think that way. I don't think anybody is that irrational in real life, are they?" The Girl replies jokingly while raising a question to the Priest's statement.

"Exactly, no one does it *in* real life, but at the same time almost everyone does it *with* their real life! Take your own example: you know what to do and hence life is opening new chapters for you each day, to take you to your goal. Otherwise who were you for me to get you out of that hell?" The Priest substantiates his point by correlating it to the mysterious objective that the girl is carrying very close to her heart.

The mere example of her own life takes the girl deep into her own thoughts where her mind has once again started pounding her heart to achieve what she is living for —the mystery purpose of her life, but why?

"But in this false reality, we, the people are slaves of the adjectives. We inadvertently keep on trying to make our life complex, which we ultimately end up defending. Because, our ego does not allow us to bow down and accept our mistakes. We all do such stupid things, just because we do not know what the actual purpose of our life is. We work but are not clear why we are working. We are working and living just to pay bills, aren't we? We worship but hardly pray. We are running in a race; not because we have to, but because we find others doing so. We are like sheep in the herd. Once our conscience starts pushing us in the right direction, we start making mistakes. Unfortunately, by that time, our ego has taken over our life. For our ego, mistakes are nothing but insults to it and insults are something the ego doesn't accept easily. What need to be in this situation? A Shepherd, not the sheep," the Priest is at his best when it comes to explaining complex things.

———————— ✦ ✦ ✦ ✦ ✦ ————————

Out there on the riverbank, some turmoil is brewing up at one of the shanty shops. People are gathering around an old TV set. Locals are hurriedly dispersing from the usually crowded bank, while pilgrims are busy in their devoting baths. Bhaijan being a local person; is curious about the situation unfolding at the corner. Something is not right in this commotion.

They sit down on the famous stone steps of the *Harish Chandra Ghaat*, with some people gathering around them with curiosity. Few people are even peeking from the funeral processions to get a glimpse of the alien girl with an Aghori. It appears as if they are mourning the loss but not yet ready to accompany the departed soul.

"I am having a very strange feeling right now," the girl speaks to herself.

She is imagining that there are people coming out of the pyres with charred bodies who then dive into the river and come out clean and pure, like gold. Sometimes she senses a lonely shadow nearby the pyre. She is completely absorbed in her thoughts and imagination.

"What is this? Have these souls done with this world or are they embarking to new world with new challenge? What's going on," are some of the thoughts floating in her mind.

She is able to impose reality and imagination in front of her. People are mingling with souls and spirits floating around them! She is in a very perceptive state: observing every movement, emotion, smell and the wind chill along with the hot sun.

The movement of people in and around the shop starts to become aggressive. Bhaijan senses some danger and hints to the Priest and the girl to board the boat immediately.

His experienced fear was right, all of a sudden, people emerge from nowhere, charging towards the riverbank with weapons in their hands.

Everyone who was in a festive mood until now has started running towards safety.

The Priest drags the girl who is still lost in her illusions, towards the boat. Breach is following them while barking furiously at the approaching mob.

The girl is still deep in her thoughts, "is it really a goal of my life? Do I really need to find Andrew? If that is the case, what am I doing here in India, sitting amongst pot smoking sannyasins and monks; watching the dead getting burned?"

Bhaijan, the Priest and the girl board the boat hurriedly, which has some heavy and strange stuff crammed inside the small cabin in it.

Breach is left behind on the riverbank. Surprisingly, the mob does not attack her.

"Adrushya Guru says; it is truly brutal but honest that a fanatic mob is nothing more than a pack of animals; maybe that's why they didn't attack their fellow, Breach," the Priest is mumbling within himself.

Finally, Breach jumps into the water and they collect her in the middle of the stream.

The girl is completely unaware of the danger she has just encountered. She shares her experience of being Kaali previous night with Bhaijan despite the objections from the Priest. For her, it has become a small family of strangers in no time! One of the reasons for this attraction may be that the language barrier is broken; another and perhaps more important reason is that these strangers in a completely alien land respect her as human. Somewhere deep in her mind she is still looking for snakes and snake charmers though.

◆ ◆ ◆ ◆ ◆ ◆

The complete shoreline of the river is burning now – not only at the funeral ground but all along the bank as well. Shops, houses, huts, small stalls, everything has been torched by the mob. It's so democratic scene out there, whoever is in majority is killing the minorities, irrespective of who is right.

Everyone is silently looking at the violence occurring at riverbank until the boat reaches a small isolated island in the middle of the river. It's here, that the girl finds out that the strange stuff in the cabin is nothing but pile of half-burned dead bodies.

Once again fear of unknown makes her aggressive and cautious. Once again, her mind is overworking to find countless ways she can fall prey to the same people she was just considering being her closest friends. We have so many ways to be afraid of death.

"Do you know we have two types of reactions to danger?" The Priest asks the girl, he is abrupt as usual in changing the topics.

"What are they?"

"Fight or Flight!" Bhaijan adds his point to the conversation; he sensed the fear in her mind perhaps.

"Right; and these two decisions are processed by two different aspects of our senses," the Priest explains. "Our brain is a 'rational stupid'. On the other hand, our mind is an 'irrational supersonic dumb'.

The brain does not look at danger as actually a danger; but as a problem. It looks at things in binary mode: a problem or its solution. It always takes any new thing happening as a problem, tries to solve it, and attempts to tackle it because that's what it is best at."

"Hmm that's interesting," the girl is a bit diverted from her thoughts.

"There has not been a single day in the last 5 years, when I haven't learnt something new from this mad scientist," Bhaijan exclaims with a chuckle.

"On the other hand, Adrushya Guru says, the mind is best at

wandering, it moves very fast; faster than light in fact!" The Priest continues while trying to catch his breath after offloading a very heavy dead body from the boat. "So, it always tries to take you to a different situation. It drags you out of conflicts. It pushes for flight from a scene as opposed to the brain, which encourages you to find the possibility to overcome the problem."

"But then why do we behave differently in different situations," interrupts the girl.

"That's our Adrushya Guru – The Master of both of these. It allows both the horses to opine and then it decides what is best in a particular situation for us," the Priest completes his theory.

"I am telling you, even when you are here on this island, thinking that these morons are talking nonsense, it is nothing but you're Adrushya Guru assisting you in deciding!" Bhaijan puts his joke in the conversation.

"Indeed, I know that you know that whatever I am saying makes sense, even though you joke about it," the Priest adds in his casual manner.

It takes almost two hours for the Priest and Bhaijan to offload the dead bodies and then put them in a big pile of wood for their second cremation. The body of an old lady is kept aside by the priest; the lower portion of it is partially burnt, but otherwise it's a healthy corpse of a woman who has died just a few hours ago. The smile on the face of mortal remains is proving the peaceful departure she had from this world. Perhaps she didn't leave anything behind to be worried about.

The Priest takes out some of his praying stuff from his bag. It includes a human skull; the sari that he offered to the girl the night before; some colors; incense sticks; and a candle.

"Some surreal things are about to happen, just don't lose your ground. Keep silent and if you can't bear the creepiness of next few moments, go back to the boat, there is a small mattress in the boat, you can go and sleep on that," the Priest warns the girl.

The Priest does an amazing job making up the body. It looks like it is almost about to talk. He whispers something in each ear of the body, sits beside it, and starts praying. His eyes are again red, like burning coal.

Even though the girl is not able to see very clearly, she can still correlate the process with what happened to her just the night before.

The Priest stands up and wildly dances around the corpse. Sometimes he shouts at the sky and on other occasions, he smiles at the body. He is always carrying a human skull filled with water with him during this process and occasionally sprinkles water from it on the body.

"Can you? Can you? Please! Please allow me, once, just once, please!" He is crying and shouting even louder at the body now. His screams are not that of anger but that of a pleading boy; a kid who is trying to persuade his mother to give him something that is otherwise dangerous in his mother's opinion.

The exhausted priest goes silent for a moment and then lights up a candle. There is a cool breeze blowing on the island but not strong enough to blow out the candle.

The Priest sits down to pray, but this time he is sitting on top of the body. The girl is shocked at what she sees as the ritual unravels. He slowly lies down over the body. The body's clothes are still intact so it does not look like a case of necrophilia, but still very weird.

To her utter dismay, the Priest slides to one side of the body and opens its blouse. Although the body appears to be fresh, still blue veins and cold flesh have already started to change the color of the skin.

The Priest abruptly takes one of the nipples in his mouth.

"SSHHH!!" Bhaijan blocks the girls from screaming by holding her mouth. "Just don't, please, just don't," he hushes her up.

The Priest's face is completely transformed. He is not looking into himself. There is a very strange innocence on his face but the girl is literally horrified.

"How in the world can a person perform foreplay on a dead body, oh my Goshh! And now, I am even less certain about what had he done with me when I was unconscious last night!" The girl is shouting within herself. She is not able to fathom even the slightest of the reality happening in front of her.

"Is he going to have sex with the body? Why is he lying there and just sucking the nipple? What a horrible and disgusting man, where is his Adrushya Guru – the epitome of principles??" Her thoughts are on wild goose chase.

Slowly and unconsciously, she adjusts herself. Realizing that she has given up, Bhaijan loses his grip on her mouth. A snake slithers out from between both legs of the girl. It stops on top of the dead body, right on its chest.

There is a small stone in the snake's mouth. It drops the stone in the half-open mouth of the corpse, resulting in a vigorously shivering body and further the Priest regaining his senses.

The exhausted snake slowly crawls down to the other side of the body and disappears in the water stream.

The Priest stands up, buttons up the blouse and takes the stone out of the body's mouth.

He again sits in front of the body and prays. This time he is crying with tears rolling down his cheeks. He looks drained, but content.

"I think his prayer is fulfilled today, it has been almost five years since he has started such rituals, but I have never seen this snake before," Bhaijan mutters some words slowly.

The Priest stands up, so does the corpse! It is a scary and beyond imagination scene on the charnel ground!

The girl can see the sweat and fear on Bhaijan's face. He is praying in his own language.

"Yah Allah, raham – be merciful!" Bhaijan is babbling within himself.

The Priest starts walking towards the big pile of bodies carefully stacked on the wood logs, followed by the body.

The girl tries to say something but nothing comes out of her throat; she wants to run away but cannot move an inch. Time, space and rationality are frozen. Fight or flight, she is not able to decide, it appears as if her brain and mind both are busy in witnessing the unfolding drama, but she is petrified. Her ability to move around is exactly same as it was last night. She could see everything as clear as crystal, but unable to react, her body has gone numb.

Bhaijan is frozen in his place. The Priest and the walking dead body enter the fire pit. The Priest turns around and bows with respect to the dead body to touch its feet – something he did with the girl last night as well. He politely directs the body to go to the center of the pit.

The body follows and moves towards the center. It drops flat as soon as it reaches the center. The Priest drops in his place, mumbling some words.

"Bhaijan!" he struggles to shout for help properly.

Bhaijan rushes to retrieve the Priest, there is a spontaneous fire in the body and entire lot starts burning quickly. Bhaijan pulls him out of the flames and pours water from skull-pot on him. The Priest struggles but slowly gets up to stand on his feet. He waves his hand towards the girl to call her. Although she is terrified, she still follows him. The mass funeral flames are reaching the sky now. The cold in the air has been taken over by the warmth and smell of burning flash from the funeral pyre.

The Priest holds her hand and gives her the stone he took out of the body's mouth. It is a small stone with a strange bluish tinge.

"Keep this with you. It is going to save someone in the blues," the Priest says.

"But remember, you can use it only once, so be wise with its use," he pauses to cough, "and also, always keep this skull with you; even after I am dead. It is going to keep you focused on your goal," he continues.

"But Pundit, you have been struggling to get this for the last 5 years, haven't you? How can you gift it to someone who is a total stranger?" Bhaijan objects to the Priest's kind gesture towards the girl.

"Bhaijan, Prophet Ibrahim sacrificed his beloved son Ismail to God, and I never said that I wanted to have this stone, I never needed anything but a goal in my life," the Priest smiles while answering and cleaning the stone upon noticing girl's disgusting look at it.

"And remember there is a subtle difference in what you want to have, and what your goal is," he looks at the girl and continues. "Look at this girl, Adrushya Guru says: she doesn't want anything, even if it is one of the world's most mysterious stones, but, she has a goal to achieve. An objective, free of desires, it is not a choice but sort of an obligation for each one of us as being a part of this universe."

"You know Pundit, I don't understand this complex logic, explain it to me in simple words," Bhaijan does not want to give up his defense.

"Do you do your Namaaz daily?" the Priest asks.

43

"Five time a day," answers Bhaijan.

"Do you fast during the month of Ramadan?"

"Since I have my memories about Islam in my mind, I have been fasting without failure."

"Is that something you want to do or you are obliged to do?"

"I am obliged to do; hence I want to do these duties," Bhaijan answers while the girl is looking at him.

"Exactly," adds the Priest with a firm voice but no emotions.

"I got it; you are talking about duties here," Bhaijan says.

"Not only duties, but duties to be performed whole heartedly." The Priest adds to his point. "It's a strange world nowadays, where people don't want to do their duties but always talk about their desires and rights." He is staring at the girl.

"They think their desires are the root of happiness, whereas it is not actually the case. True happiness is in fulfilling one's role; in completing one's task in this world, because true happiness is a by-product of the satisfaction that we get upon achieving something. Also, some say happiness is what we feel when we get something that we want. It is actually an ephemeral outcome of the excitement – and that is just not happiness – it is simply not. This false happiness is like the exit point of the rollercoaster: when you are still sitting in the wagon, you realize you have beaten death but still do not know what is next. The moment you come out of it, you realize the toll you have taken on your body, your soul." He is struggling to walk properly.

◆ ◆◆◆◆ ◆

The girl's fear and disgust disappears slowly and she helps the lymping Priest to walk properly. Breach is following them, while holding the skull in her mouth carefully.

The fire is at its peak. Bhaijan and the Priest are sitting beside and weeping slowly. Their tears are rolling out silently as-if these teardrops are aware of their destiny and have already given up any hope to remain inside the eyes.

--- ANAHATA ---
(THE UNBEATEN VOYAGE)

It is late in the evening and the mass funeral fire is a little bit calmer. Bhaijan and the Priest stand up; give each other a warm hug and help the girl to board the boat along with Breach.

The Priest has some bells in his hands, which he has taken from one of the corpses.

The girl is still lost in the sequence of events unfolded in the past few hours. Eternity has unraveled a very different and mystical world in front of her that she had never thought of witnessing even in her wildest of the dreams.

"But then, why is all of this happening to me? Am I missing the right path? Am I simply pushing myself towards my destination subconsciously? How is it connected with my quest of life? No one seems to know the answer.

I still know what my job, my obligation, in this world is and I am very clear about that. But, how to do it? Where is Andrew? How to find him?

How can I get out of this peculiar and unknown situation and move back to my country to restart my search?" A storm is brewing in her brain with so many questions about her goal and the way to achieve it.

———————— ✦✦✦✦✦✦ ————————

She is imagining herself dressed like Kaali again. This illusion is becoming more frequent for her now, an image very similar to the one she had seen the night before – her alter image dressed in gaudy dress with angry face; with skull in one hand and a heavy dagger in the other.

"You don't know how to swim, right?" Her Kaali form asks her. She is daydreaming with her eyes wide open.

"Right, I never learnt how to swim."

"Then jump in the water and test yourself. Test your goal, check your destiny," Kaali orders her. "If you don't have a desire but a duty to be fulfilled, you must learn to give it up, even if it is your life," she continues with her amber eyes spitting red flames. "And, if you don't jump in the water now, then it means you still have desires in your mind and you are afraid for your life instead of being committed to your destiny."

"It is just too much in the last two days! I can't handle it anymore!" The girl shouts back at the Kaali.

"Then you are not ready, you simply want to go back to prostitution. You are heading to your alternate success. You want to die daily instead of living a moment and then moving on to the next one alive!

But, I will assure you one thing here, you have a destiny and I have brought you thus far in the quest of achieving it. There is no choice left with you anymore. You have gone through so much pain and agony to get me at your side. If you want to leave in the middle now, it is going to break the balance of your universe, and I am not going to let that happen."

I can leave you forever but only in one condition: that you clearly define what you want in your life and abandon your goal," Kaali tells her.

"What do you suggest?" the girl tries to play a trick.

"Do what you are best at," Kaali says.

"And that is?" the girl does not stop.

"You know that is! Just believe in that," Kaali answers cleverly.

The loud noise of splashing water diverts the Priest and Bhaijan's attention from the burning city.

The girl is nowhere on the boat. They look down the river and see her struggling to float in the water.

"I need to save her or else Americans will declare me a terrorist!" Bhaijan readies to jump in it.

"Hold on, it's the turning point of her and our lives, let her realize it." The Priest stops him from diving in the water.

"Remember, true knowledge is what you can apply in the real world. All the inspirations; all the motivations simply don't matter if they don't give any insight into life when you need it most," Kaali is still speaking with the girl who is fighting for her life inside the water. "In theory, you know very well that when you can't swim, when you feel that you don't have control over yourself, just floating is enough to survive, but can you do that now, when you are actually in the water?" Kaali is instigating her to think positive in such a distressed situation.

The girl is exhausted; she is slowly giving up her efforts to swim in the water. Fear is dangerously caving in her mind to let go. It seems as if someone or something inside her is asking her to lose the battle of selfishness. On the other hand, Kaali from the outside is inspiring her to fight the war of selflessness.

Kaali comes closer to the girl and holds her hands from fluttering in the water. She puts her hand on the girl's nose and mouth to stop her from drinking water. The girl is calm now; a sense of someone holding her hand breathes new life into her sinking confidence. She is relaxed, so is the water around her and she starts floating in it like a leaf.

"See, it is so simple! Just give up the idea that you actually need to follow the traditional way of struggle to survive. Give up the idea that you are going to die; give up the thought: what if you cannot survive. Just try to live for a moment. Even if death is knocking at your door – try to live the death. I can assure you, it will be surprised by your attitude," Kaali whispers in her ears.

The girl is on the surface of the water. She is floating with the current now.

"Do not worry, I am with you and will always be with you unless you stop hearing from me, or you stop paying attention to me," Kaali says and disappears.

"Can somebody pull me back into the boat? It's very comfortable but a little cold out here in the water," the girl shouts laughingly with her voice mixed with water.

"She has just passed one of the toughest lessons of her life. It is going to help her in very difficult situations not too far away in the future. Be ready for our final journey Bhaijan, now we are part of her voyage," the mesmerized Priest says.

Bhaijan steers the boat towards her and pulls her in it.

"Why did you jump in the water? You should have asked me for water if you were thirsty," Bhaijan cracks a joke with an emotional voice.

"My Adrushya Guru says: if you can't swim, just float in the water. Don't be afraid – water will be your best friend!" She answers smilingly,

"So I thought of challenging my fear. And I can tell you – my fear is really afraid of me now!"

All three breaks into laughter, before settling down on the boat.

The bells on Breach's legs are ringing in no particular rhythm and the girl is staring at Breach playing with the Priest.

The girl is still looking at the Priest with disgust. She is still wondering why someone would even think of necrophilia. For her, the Priest is a sick psycho! He had full opportunity to have sex with her but preferred to play and sleep with a dead body.

"She was my mother, like you are!" The Priest shouts in anger at the girl, as if he has read her mind. "I was not having sex with her but trying to sleep, as a baby does with his mother. I was sleeping with her to realize how close we are to the ultimate reality."

"Have you ever seen a very young child?" he asks.

"You mean a baby or an infant? Yes, I have."

"Do they ever know what is dirty what is not?" The Priest is digging in his heels, "Can they distinguish between good and bad? Can they differentiate between truth and lies?" His voice is loud now. "No, they can't, and that's the ultimate power; the power of Innocence! If we can retain or regain this power when we grow up, we can get anything in this world. That's the power of a hundred percent efficient machines."

He pauses to look at the huge fire on the bank of the river. "And you may even notice this in the current mechanical world as well: you see a new born kid, what power he has?"

"Nothing, he can't speak, walk or even indicate what he wants. He has no way to explain what he is seeing or even what his feelings are. But he has the ultimate power, the fantastic way to communicate – his innocence – through which he connects himself to his mother or father," he is calm again.

"We are in a purest state of prayers whenever we are taking care of such babies, because, we are listening to the language of the Almighty, because we are working without any expectations from those kids. We respond to their thoughts, because we are able to listen to it. This power in babies comes from their equanimity. They look at everything with the same point of view, they don't have duality."

"Do you know the only body part kids start to use to learn new things, is the tongue? I cannot say if they use it to taste, feel or see, but each and every thing by default goes in their mouth and then they start to look at it."

"I am neither a psychologist nor a scientist," the girl counters pertly.

Bhaijan laughs at this point while looking the other way to steer the boat.

"Well, maybe some won't agree with this statement but that's a different story. I am not limiting myself to logic here," the Priest says.

"But, when I am praying with a dead body, I am trying to make myself like a baby, who doesn't have any distinction. Everything is acceptable with open arms, because once I achieve this stage, I am certain I will be able to experience the supreme.

"I slept with a dead body like a baby does with his mother but it is you who saw it differently. It doesn't matter that what others think – what matters is that what I feel," he continues, "If we cannot interfere and ask someone to mend their way, we should also not have an opinion about that person."

"Anyway, coming back to that seemingly necromantic ritual, what I was doing is called Aghora – Beyond Extreme – it means there is nothing like: bad, fear, disgust, hate, darkness or any other adjective in this world. It is eternal joy within you, it is endless, just like kids think." The Priest says his last statement with a very composed smile.

"The person who performs Aghora is called an Aghori," Bhaijan gives his input.

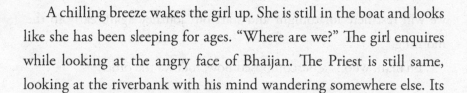

"I have made Breach a little bit more 'visible' for your ears now," the Priest changes the topic.

Bhaijan, who still does not know that the girl is partially blind, shakes his head in frustration. "Sometimes, too much knowledge of anything is very dangerous. Now I can't figure it out and neither do I want to anyway, that how the hell you are going to see from your ears," he is complaining about the seemingly irrational statement made by the priest.

However, the girl who knows what the Priest means, is feeling relaxed after a long time, resulting in her falling asleep.

It's dark and moonlight is spreading fast across the banks of the river.

A chilling breeze wakes the girl up. She is still in the boat and looks like she has been sleeping for ages. "Where are we?" The girl enquires while looking at the angry face of Bhaijan. The Priest is still same, looking at the riverbank with his mind wandering somewhere else. Its dark in the night, there are no signs of the burning city now.

"We are in the boat," Bhaijan says with a hollow voice.

"I understand that I am not in Titanic, but are we still around Banaras? I am hungry! When will we be reaching the riverbank?" The girl replies indifferently to Bhaijan's anger.

53

"Maybe in fourteen days," Bhaijan replies.

"What?" Now she is angry.

She jumps in the water straight away while grabbing her bag on the way. This reaction shows that she still has the fear of the unknown and is hesitant to believe what she hears.

This is what human beings have learnt and distorted during their evolution. Every moment is a new one so why carry over trust from history; the best weapon in this world is mistrust. Never believe anyone blindly. Alas! We – the intelligentsia!

She unsuccessfully tries to swim through the cold and strong water current.

"Come back in the boat, I will explain it to you," the Priest who is sitting with Breach orders her.

She realizes that it is not possible for her to swim and get to the riverbank; and even if she does, it would be impossible to find the way out of the bushes without the help of Breach.

The Priest helps her to board the boat. She is completely drenched but there are no clothes to change into.

"Bhaijan, take the boat to the bank, we are very near to city now, we will rest here for tonight and start our journey again early in the morning."

Bhaijan, who is a bit composed now, follows the order.

Once at the bank, Bhaijan gives an outfit of his own clothes to the girl to change into. She does not mind changing in front of them but both men simply turn away and become busy in lighting the fire.

Two big cross-like cut marks are clearly visible on the girl's chest. She, in spite of looking like a perfect girl, does not have breasts. The cross-marks show the brutality she must have gone through in her unknown and evidently dark past.

She is surprised to see the food supply available on the boat.

"Where did you get all this from?" She asks.

The fire is at its peak now.

"Let's talk about this now," the Priest says.

Bhaijan is looking at the Priest's bag. All three of them are sitting in a circle around the fire.

Bhaijan is busy cooking while the Priest is mumbling some chants.

"Well, we went back to the city. There we found out that the other prostitutes from your brothel have revolted and Mausi, the head-mistress is blaming you for that. Her goons ransacked my already-shabby hut and still searching for us in the whole city. So, we left you in the boat, as you were sleeping, and prepared to leave the city."

"So, what's next?" She asks.

"I don't know," the Priest replies.

"We are travelling by boat to Kolkata now, to drop you at the US embassy there. How much money do you have?"

The girl looks inside her soaked bag and finds about five thousand Indian Rupees.

"I have this much," she hands over the money to the Priest.

The Priest empties his bag in which there are few sketches in the bundle of papers. One of them is of Breach and another one is of the girl.

"What the heck! When did you make these new ones?" Bhaijan almost shouts at the Priest while comparing the sketches with the girl and Breach.

"What?" the girl asks, she can partially see the papers in the bright flames coming out of the fire, for her those are just rough sketches of a girl and a dog; they do look familiar though.

There is another one of a castle like building with a mountain in the background and sentries at the gate. It flies and falls right in the middle of the fire leading to a bright impression by the flames of the drawing. The burning images are clearly visible to the girl like a carving in gold.

"What is that castle?" She shoots a question to the Priest.

Bhaijan picks up the other two sketches and puts them in the flames right in front of the girl. The position of three images is such that it looks like the girl and Breach are standing in front of the castle.

"What's that all about? How did you get my sketches and especially those from when I was really young?" She shouts at the Priest and stands up to run away. As she tries to pick up her bag, Breach pulls her back from running away.

"Are you Joan?" Bhaijan asked.

"Holy hell!! How do you know my name?" the girl is shocked, "Nobody in this part of the world knows my name, I haven't heard anybody say my name in ages!" The girl is a bit scared on one hand and relaxed on the other. Now that her name is out, she feels more determined towards her goal. It may be that her obscure identity was holding her commitment towards her self-defined destiny.

A long conversation ensues over dinner. Bhaijan explains the importance of the river Ganga and its impact on Indian society irrespective of religion or beliefs of the people living on its bank.

Joan sleeps in the boat with Breach; the Priest and Bhaijan spend the night on the bank by the fireside.

It is very early morning when Joan wakes others up to get going.

Their boat starts sailing along the river. Bhaijan has switched off the engine once boat is midstream as it is still dark and they do not want to come in view of the police patrols.

The sun is slowly rising ahead of them so does the activities in the river. There are lots of fishing boats while some other are just taking passengers across the river.

As the silent day progresses on the boat, the clatter in the mind of three passengers starts to grow.

"Bhaijan, if I am not mistaken, you know how to teach fishing to dogs, don't you?"

"Pundit, do you want to eat fish now?" Bhaijan jokes.

"No, while we are moving towards Kolkata, let's do something good. Let's teach fishing to Breach," the Priest suggests.

"That's a good idea," the girl and Bhaijan agree together.

Bhaijan picks up a small piece of bread and sticks it on the tip of Breach's nose, and throws her in the water.

It happens so quickly that Joan hardly gets a chance to react. She is screaming, "What did you just do? Pull her back; she will drown in the strong current!"

It takes two minutes for Breach to struggle in the water and when Bhaijan pulls her out, she has many small bites on her face. It looks like the fish were biting her as they pulled bread out of her nose.

"What the hell?" the girl is angry with Bhaijan and the Priest. "Do you think this is a joke?"

The others are laughing silently.

"One needs to go through pain if one really wants to learn something in this world," the Priest says lightly. "Otherwise, one will never know the value of that knowledge," Bhaijan and the Priest speak together.

"I don't care, I only have one living thing that I can blindly rely on, and that is Breach," the girl is in no mood to let it go.

"And we want to take her to the next level. We should always keep learning, each moment. If we live even a single day without learning something, then it is a waste of that day in our life. This is equally applicable to animals too."

Breach spits out a small fish from her mouth.

"Masha-Allah Breach!" Bhaijan chuckles with delight.

"Wow! Did you really catch a fish just now? Unbelievable," the girl hugs her.

"If you don't mind, I can teach her the perfect way of catching fish from the water."

"But she doesn't even know how to swim," the girl is a bit calmer now and intently considering the possibilities. A great non-physical entity, the grand and mysterious mind is again at work – to find possibilities instead of logic. It is so true that it's only possibilities that force people to find the logic behind them.

"How do you know she can't swim?" the Priest asks her.

"I never taught her how to swim," the girl answers.

"Do you know, in this world, all living beings except humans are good swimmers by birth?" Bhaijan adds to his point, "No, I didn't," says the girl.

"Except human beings, no animal is afraid of water and neither are they audacious with it, so water always gives them the way to live with it, and in return they respect the existence of water. Result?" The priest pauses to look at the girl, who nods her head in quest of the answer.

"Even a snake without any limbs can swim for miles without getting tired," the Priest completes his point.

"Okay, it is worth to pass time while we are travelling to the next big city, where I can go and meet with US consulate officials. By the way, what is the name of the city?"

"We are approaching Patna now, but the next city where we have the US consulate is in Kolkata. It will take another five days to reach Kolkata from here."

Three police boats are approaching them. They are looking like security guards.

The Priest, Bhaijan and the leader of the people on the police boat have a long conversation.

"He is asking if you are an Indian or a foreigner." Bhaijan comes to the girl and asks.

"Tell the truth, I am who I am, maybe these guys will help us reach Kolkata much quickly," the girl responds optimistically.

"And what are you doing here?" Bhaijan counters her.

"What a whore does anywhere?" The girl answers sarcastically. "I know what they are looking for, let me go and talk to them," she moves towards the gathered people.

"Don't you see from my face that I am a whore? My name is B-Cube; do you know what that means?" The girl pauses for a moment

"It means: Bastard Blind Bitch," she completes her name.

"Huh, you must be joking," The officer in the group rejects her claim, "Let's go, we don't want to waste your time with them."

"Come with us to the police station," he drags the girl along with them.

"Tell me what you want?" the Priest interferes, and finds the butt of a country-made rifle land on his head instantly.

"No!! Don't do anything to them, let's go, I can give you one hour, it is worth 2500 Rupees of pleasure," the Girl tells him.

They change boats; the girl takes her bag along with her.

The girl emerges out of the small cabin in the boat in about fifteen minutes.

"Don't disturb your boss. He is in the heavens right now," she advises the guards in a very commanding voice.

They laugh at her tired walking.

"He also said we should all leave while he takes a breather after such intense sex-ercise," she tells them jokingly.

"Let me ask him," one of the guards stops her from leaving the boat.

"You dare? But don't blame me afterwards," the girl tries to discourage him but the guard is already peeking inside the cabin.

"Okay, looks like, sir hasn't experienced such a thing in his life. He really IS in the heavens now!" The guard jokes and everyone, including the girl, join him in laughter.

"Can I go now," She asks impatiently.

"What about us," One of the guards asks.

"Get permission from your boss. You guys are vultures, you will have to wait until I die," the girl taunts on their slave-like attitude.

One of the sensible and elderly guards on the boat allows her to leave. By this time, Bhaijan and the Priest have realized that they have to leave as soon as possible. Their boat is ready to move.

"Remember, he is really at peace right now, tasting the juices of the heavens, so don't bother to wake him up, until he is completely out of my dreams!"

The girl shouts amid the loud noise of the boat engine. Their boat speeds off as soon as she finishes her last word.

"Did you kill him?" The Priest asks the girl. "Maybe, I am not sure, is he a police officer?"

"No, that's the only thing in our favor; he was just a local thug, disguised as a policeman," Bhaijan tells her.

"Then move fast and get out of their area as soon as possible," the girl screams at him. Their boat speeds off the scene before the guards on the boat can discover the reason for them speeding off.

Bhaijan switches off the boat and maneuvers it along with the strong current as they enter the main stream. The Priest and Bhaijan take turns managing the steering of the rusted handle of the boat.

"Why are you guys not sailing fast?" the girl starts to feel a bit impatient.

"Ohh dear Kaali, just don't push yourself to the brink," the Priest says while kneeling in front of her. "Aim is always to reach the destination but the path traversed to reach the end is also equally vital. The lessons of the path make us eligible to consume the energy of the success upon reaching the destination."

"If you achieve the goal, then you have the experience of success. However, when you travel on the road to the goal; you experience yourself," Bhaijan adds to the Priest's point and announces, "We will be passing the banks of Nalanda shortly."

"What is Nalanda?" the girl asks curiously. There are some distant clay mounds visible from the boat.

"Those ruins are the perfect example of achieving the goal without experiencing the road to those goals," the Priest says.

"I don't get it," the girl asks for elaboration.

"Nalanda is the birthplace of current day mathematics. The Great ancient Indian Saint Aryabhatta discovered "Zero" right here in this great alma mater of scholars," the Priest tells her.

"And, regarding your question about how it correlates with the path versus goal analogy: this is the place, later conquered by a ruler who didn't know what he had just achieved; resulting in an irreversible loss to humanity," Bhaijan says. "An idiotic, tyrant and moron who didn't know what books are meant for. He didn't even know what the Holy Quran says about books; he got this town of scholars as a reward after winning a battle. He broke the unwritten rule of war in the Indian subcontinent to not attack shelters and education centers just to satisfy personal ego."

"Bhaijan, is it you who is saying this?" the Priest wonders. "I have never heard you saying anything against fellow Muslims."

"Being Muslim is not always being right; being Muslim is not always being human. To human is to err," Bhaijan says. "I am more an Indian than a Muslim, and, even more a human than an Indian or Muslim. I have no constraint from my conscience, which is my religion to call a spade a spade," Bhaijan continues while looking at the mounds.

"The dictator who destroyed this temple of education, the baseline of Al-Baruni's work on mathematics, didn't know what he was doing. He only had one thing in his mind, and that was the sword, which he used at its best. He attacked Nalanda University by mistaking it to be a fort, full of treasures. Once he realized that it is a university, he burnt the whole campus in anger! Had he attended any school, he would have known what treasure was hidden in the books; had he ever experienced himself as a student, the story would have been different," Bhaijan further explains. "This is what happens when we achieve goals, without knowing their value for us, or our society,"

"That's a very true and fascinating explanation of this simple thing in life called – the journey," the Priest responds.

"I get it. However, I have a long way to go and there is a lot to learn in this small and uncertain life. Every page of my life is being turned over as if it is the last one," says the girl, who is completely lost in watching the water stream.

"And that's the way it should be," the Priest chuckles. "So Bhaijan, tell me what else can you explain about Islam?"

"Wait, Bhaijan are you a Muslim?" the girl asks curiously.

"Do you know about Muslims?" Bhaijan asks laughingly.

"Yeah, my mother was half Muslim," the girl reveals. "She was not regular in her practices but very devoted to her belief."

"May be that's why she used to call her brother Bhaijan," she continues. "I was always curious to know about her beliefs, because of her frequent arguments with my father who was a staunch Catholic, over their religious beliefs."

"I am sure you would have heard a few words like: Qafir, Quran, Allah, and Muhammad (peace be upon him)," Bhaijan offers his opinion.

"Yeah, she used to call my father a Qafir and many times it even led to violent fights between them," the girl agrees to his point. "But I couldn't discuss this with her, because she passed away before I was mature enough to talk about these things."

"Hah – Qafir – an adjective, which itself says if it exists; so do the people with this characteristic." Bhaijan is speaking while staring at the horizon. "Although Islam is one of the very few religions that is holding its original values intact, still it is perhaps the most widely misinterpreted one."

"Principles of other religions have had their periodic reviews; be it due to political or spiritual or may be even practical reasons. The rules of living a disciplined life keeps changing according to the time. These changes in the rules keep people in their confidence zone. This dynamics in rules also keep them free of sins psychologically."

"The same act that was a sin in the past, say two hundred years ago; is not a sin anymore. Earlier people were hung to death when they did some forbidden acts; in today's world those very acts are defined as venerable, and not only society but religious leaders confer that recognition to people."

"Bhaijan, I want to learn about Islam before I can compare it with any other religion," the girl interrupts him. " And, I am an atheist actually. So, this learning is nothing but a factual attempt to know something instead of boasting the superiority of my nonexistent faith."

"Yeah you are right, the root cause of all the troubles in this world is due to these bloody comparisons only. 'I am better than anyone else'; this thought is the reason of all the destructions in the world," Bhaijan agrees with her.

As the boat crosses an old bridge, the passengers can clearly see some rioters pushing helpless people from the bridge into the river. Riots are the tussle of dominance between small mobs and bigger mobs; the former leaves the faces of victims and the latter leaves a faceless trail of brutalities behind them. We just try to associate it with the known social adjectives, whereas riots are nothing more than animal instincts of humans.

"To understand Islam, we must first talk about one simple thing – What is not Islam; and anyone who does not follow Islam's fundamental tenets. Because when we know what is not, then, we by default know what it is. The Pundit calls it: weeding out the wrong choices to find the only right option."

"Qafirs or apostates are the ones who do not follow Islam, so the question is: who are Qafirs?"

"Anybody who doesn't believe in the teachings of Quran-e-Sharif is a Qafir."

"And, what are the teachings of the Quran-e-Sharif?"

"La-Ilahe-Ill-Allah. That's the most fundamental teaching of the Quran."

"What does that mean," the girl asks

"Eko-wa-advitiyam-Na-asti," the Priest spontaneously adds.

"And what does that mean??" The girl is even more confused.

"There is one and only one God, nobody else," Bhaijan answers.

"But that's exactly same what we say in Christianity as well," the girl claims.

"But you said you are atheist," the Priest comments on her earlier statement.

"Yeah, I am, but still had to attend mass during my childhood. Nevertheless, that is not the point here. I am talking about similar messages in different and adverse religions," the girl clarifies.

"True, they are all adverse to each other." Bhaijan admits. "So, Islam in one statement is 'there is no God other than Allah. And whoever doesn't believe in this statement, is a Qafir.'"

The rest of the pillars of Islam are just solidifications of this fundamental belief, this confession to the ultimate Supreme.

You perform 'Namaaz' five times a day to remind yourself that there is no other God but Allah.

You donate alms to demonstrate that Allah has given you not only this life but also the power of thinking and you recognize this by mimicking it's way by giving all that is precious to you not the leftover

You fast during the month of Ramadan to demonstrate that there are more important things in this world than just eating and sleeping. For that purpose, God has created other forms of life.

So, to summarize, believing that there is just one God and bringing discipline in your life to experience that supreme power is Islam."

"But you have pilgrimage as well amongst the five pillars of Islam, don't you?" The Priest is a curious and ardent disciple right now.

"Well, it was introduced later on and has a very positive socio-political influence," Bhaijan explains further.

"Quran-e-Sharif is the fundamental book to follow in Islam; it was revealed by the Almighty to Mohammad Paigamber, peace be upon him, so it is childish to say that he had written that one of the pillars of Islam is to visit his highness's own tomb.

It was added subsequently from a social point of view to bring the whole Muslim community to one place and unite them to one objective – an ideal of selfless.

Otherwise, for a true Muslim, it is very similar to Idol worship. Ultimately you are submitting to a physical object, even if it is a holiest one"

The girl is listening attentively and also paying attention to the silent music of the water. "But I heard my mom saying that Idol worshipers are the Qafirs," she asks for clarification.

"True, Idol worship is actually strictly forbidden in Islam," Bhaijan is steering the wheel now, and seems to be steering the conversation as well as the faith of the other passengers.

"Consider this rationale: Islam says there is no God but Allah, but now if I say this small statue or this small tomb or that big mountain or even the river Ganga is God then as per scientific boundaries, this object must be within some other object, or space, or time.

Now if this so-called God is confined within some other object then that object is bigger than God. Hence, its singularity is gone, so is the faith in a unique, unambiguous God.

This breaks the most fundamental tenet called God into pieces, which then causes chaos; this chaos further results in doubt and finally in disbelief."

"What does Islam say about reincarnation, spiritual uplifting and behavior?" the Priest asks Bhaijan.

"Wait, before we move to the corner of intellectuals, I have some more queries here," the girl interrupts and starts with her next question before waiting for anyone else's response to her misdemeanor.

"Then there must not be any Qafir in this world, as all of the religions have the same interpretation of God," the girl counters them.

"Let me ask you a quick question about yourself, this may help in answering your question," the Priest pitches in.

"Go ahead," the girl opens up for debate.

"What was your opinion about India before we started talking about India? Was it one of a land of snake charmers?" the Priest asks.

"Yeah," the girl replies

"And then it converted to be that of rapists who were exploiting you sexually in the brothel?" he continues.

"Of course, I didn't meet any other type of people until I met you guys," she further answers.

"And subsequently you got an impression of us being cannibals or nomads or even illiterates until very recently?" another question by the Priest.

"Agreed," the girl speaks shyly.

"And during all this time you were comparing people with the benchmark you had set up since your childhood in your country.

Now if you stop changing your mind and always say that your point of view is always right and it is going to be right forever, then, it becomes an issue," Bhaijan comments on her opinions.

"You cannot wear a wild goose jacket in the winters of India, can you? You will die sweating in this weather. At the same time, one cannot go to New York and take a dip in the Hudson River on January 14th as they do here in India," the Priest says jokingly.

"The singularity of God is common in all religions but – my way of achieving this Singularity is better than yours – this duality is the root cause of all adversity," Bhaijan is at his best in explaining his point of view.

◆ ◆ ◆ ◆ ◆ ◆

'Boom!' a loud deafening noise drags their attention to the other side of the bank. There is an explosion in the boat passing by theirs.

"Allah-U-Akbar; Allah-U-Akbar!" Some people in the other boats are celebrating.

"Ten Qafirs have been sent to hell to burn in the fire of ignorance!" their leader shouts.

Some of the dinghies from the gang are accosting towards the Bhaijan's boat.

"Just remember what I have told you guys about Islam, if you believe in the singular supreme God, then say it in Arabic, and let the truth prevail. I may or may not be able to help you guys but I can assure you this: it will be I martyred before either one of you is harmed," Bhaijan moves towards the corner where the leader's boat is approaching. "And that's the promise of a Muslim-in-quest-of-Allah."

Three dinghies dock from the front to block the escape route and the leader of the group jumps in the passengers' boat. He is wearing a skullcap and has the typical Muslim look with fiery eyes. As soon as he is on board, others from his gang jump aboard and take their position to surround the passengers.

"As-salamu-alaykum Mia," Bhaijan greets him.

He ignores the greeting and moves straight towards the girl.

68

"Who are you?" He shouts at the girl.

"A girl."

A tight slap lands on her face as soon as her eyes meet those of the leader's. She falls down. Within no time, Breach is all over the leader who was not expecting a dog to attack. He does not even get the chance to take out his sword or knife.

The girl recovers herself and pulls Breach from further attacking the bloodied leader.

The leader lunges at Breach with his sword but Bhaijan stops him in the middle.

"I said 'As-salamu-alaykum Mia. Where is your qaida (Manners)?" Bhaijan says something in the leader's ears that calms him down.

"But, if they are not Muslims, I am going to drop their heads right here on your boat," he shouts all of a sudden.

"But when did I say they are Muslims, I said they are not Qafirs and they are on the path of devotion, Insha'Allah very soon," Bhaijan reverts in a relatively slow but firm voice.

"What is the Supreme Confession?" The leader shouts at the Priest.

"La-Ilahe-e-Ill-Allah."

"Why do you have these big hair and moustaches? Are you a Sadhu, speaking Qalma just due to fear of impending death?" He further enquires.

"I was trying to be an Aghori until recently," the Priest is also firm in answering.

Two of the gang members charge at the Priest while shouting. "You Cannibals, you don't even have the right to live!"

However, they freeze where they are.

The Priest moves towards them with a very calm smile.

"Why do you think, I do not have right to live? Even if I say La-Ilahe-e-Ill-Allah, I still don't?" Everyone on the boat is shocked.

"Until today, I was trying to be an Aghori, but today I have become a true Aghori, and many thanks to Bhaijan, who guided me up to this final milestone. Otherwise I would have died with my definition of the duality in God," the Priest explains. "You cannot even touch us, because it is his wish," He points to sky. The moment he turns around the two of the charging gang members, drop dead on the floor.

"I am a follower of the singularity of God; call it Allah or God or Ishwar. I have one Aghora view of those," he moves towards the leader. "Now let me know how else I will have to prove myself to be a Muslim – A Faithful?"

The leader drops his weapon and asks Bhaijan. "Where are you guys going?"

"Kolkata," Bhaijan responds.

"This girl doesn't look like an Indian, who is she?" he continues his question.

"She is asking to go to America but you are right she is not an Indian, we got her freed from a brothel in Banaras," the Priest tells him.

"Ohh, is she B-CUBE?" he asks for confirmation.

"Yes," Bhaijan answers.

"There are many gangs looking for her," he pauses before continuing further. "Is she seriously a Muslim?"

"She believes in confession but not yet a Muslim, her mother was a half Muslin though."

"Which country do you belong to?" the leader shouts at the girl.

"United States of America," the girl replies, there is a strange power of truth prevailing amongst the unarmed passengers and that is leaving the armed attackers powerless.

"So here is the deal, I let you guys continue, you can even have a better boat, but, leave her with us," the leader puts his condition.

"Brother, we don't game on the powerless, especially girls," the Priest opposes his idea.

"Then no one is leaving from here, the Qafir will be killed because that is my duty towards my faith, and you people will be butchered because you are aiding a Qafir," the leader spills his plan and lunges towards the girl.

To the Priest and Bhaijan's shock, the girl, who is prepared this time, kicks him with such ferocity that the leader falls straight off the boat.

"Is there anyone else, who wants to kill a believer, I have seen a lot of blood in my life, even drunk it once!" Bhaijan picks up the leader's sword and joins the girl in challenging the goons.

"Let me check who is a real believer here," a rocky voice comes from the cabin of the mother-boat.

An elderly, six-foot-tall man with a strong built comes out of the cabin. He has his face covered with the side of his turban.

"What is the supreme confession?" He approaches the girl directly and asks her.

"Don't you know?" The girl retorts without fear.

"I know, but if you don't tell me, I won't be able to judge you and in which case you are just an American to me," he tries to convince her reluctantly.

"Who are you to judge me and my faith?" The girl is in no mood to relent, moreover, she is feeling much stronger to defeat her enemy in an argument.

"OK, what is your faith?" The person asks her again.

"I think you should tell him," the Priest interrupts.

The elderly man turns around to look at the Priest. They bow their heads to each other in respect.

"There is no God but one and that is Allah," the girl follows the Priest's advice.

"Subhan-Allah, and what are the five pillars of Islam?" He asks another question.

"Why should we limit ourselves to two or three or even five aspects when we know there is nothing, no one, but only God?" The girl shoots a screaming question back to him. "Why can't we simply follow the ultimate supreme being instead of following rules?" Her voice is even more firm and her logic is enough to shake the faith of the other gang members.

"But there must be a way, defined by wise men, which we should follow to achieve the goal of the religion," the elderly person furthers the argument.

"Aha! that's the problem I think, thanks for this invaluable insight of the mind of a believer!" The girl chuckles with an eye-to-eye gaze with the elderly person. Her dress is a bit disheveled and her almost nonexistent cleavage is visible out of the contrasting color blouse. The elderly person looks away to avoid the distraction.

"You didn't ask me to define my goal, but to define what I think is right, and, I think we don't practice to achieve what is already right. But, we practice, or in other words we aspire to practice with commitment to become close to *that* Right, the Alone and Supreme."

"I agree with your point, Mohtarma; can you please cover your body properly?" A slightly conforming elderly requests the girl to cover her chest properly with the sari she has on.

"Why?" The girl shoots back at him with no sign of giving up her upper hand in the argument.

"Your clothes are distracting me." The elderly person confesses.

"No, I am not distracting you with my body, or with my clothes. But, it is the lack of commitment; the missing singularity; the insufficient dedication to the confession that is distracting you. I am what I am, my body is what it is, how can it distract you?" The girl responds.

"Do you never look at your mother? What are your feelings at that time? Why are those feelings different when looking at any other girl's breasts?" The girl mocks him.

"I think we are deviating from our original discussion," the elderly man counters her in order to move back to the original discussion. "Let's move to the point, what do you practice to be a devout Muslim?"

"I don't think we are deviating, it is part of a Muslim's Wazoo – the Ablutions I guess. Anyway, I do not practice anything to be a Muslim, but I try to be a Muslim –a Faithful. As I understand, if there is just one God and nothing else, I don't think anyone can be a Qafir in this world. We have people who believe and then we have people who don't know what to believe in, ultimately, they also believe in something which is just a different form of the absolute belief. The difference may be in terms of language, perception or the path they are trying to follow," the girl is all over the elderly man now. His fellow men are looking nervous; some are tightening their helpless grips on their swords to attempt an already failed attack on the girl.

"I don't do Namaaz, because I don't know how to do it. I don't give Alms, because I don't have anything to give, but I can assure you that I have given up my whole life to one goal which I think serves my purpose in this world.

Do I have any plans to visit Mecca? No, because I think the Supreme One is all around us, and if that is the case, Mecca will be right here in this boat one day. Why should I keep wandering? I promise you, one day I will have Macqa right here in the boat!

I don't fast because I hardly eat on regular days," the girl provides details of why she doesn't practice the five pillars the elderly man questioned her about.

"This guy, the Priest called me mother even though I am younger than him. He thinks if he needs to find God, he needs to sleep with dead, he needs to suck the breast of a rotten corpse, he needs to smoke pot and meditate all day," the girl points towards the priest.

"I was an atheist until this morning, even up to a while ago, but now I am a believer; just a believer not a follower of any particular faith. Because, perfection to be the ultimate cannot come by practice, but, by purification only, and it comes by living with the commitment to it at each and every moment." The girl clearly shows that she is no nonsense and that her words have meaning and experience for the audience on the boat.

"Now what? Are you going to kill me, just because I don't follow your way to be with my ultimate soul; who is the same for you and me, provided both of us believe in singularity?" The girl stares into the eyes of the elderly man. "Then do it now, I will be more than happy to depart from this place. It may be that the goal of my life is to become food for some hungry fish in this river, and maybe you are just instrumental in this process."

"But then you are saying: let others do whatever they think is right without telling them what is actually right?" The elderly man is a curious student of the girl now.

"*What is* actually 'right'?" The Girl asks him at the same time she kneels to sip some water from the river. A few Ganga dolphins are diving around the boats in search of food.

"Allah," the elderly man replies in one word.

"That's right, Allah is the One, and It has a plan for each one of us and that plan clearly doesn't say that just because someone is pretending not to believe in It, to kill him."

"We still need to follow some rules and guidelines to walk on the path of God. You cannot drive on the road without following traffic rules. Those rules may be rules of the land or rules defined by souls who have experienced His Highness," the Priest puts in his point of view.

"How do you know that the Supreme is a 'His Highness'? Not a 'Her Highness'?" The girl counters him.

"I am sorry, it's the Highest-ness," the Priest corrects himself. "If we don't know where to go, then the path to the goal will be like a jungle."

"Agreed, but this road of belief must be an individual's private path. There is no perfect fit formula for everybody," the girl adds to his point. "So, why should I follow the rules given by others? The rules confuse me more, instead of giving me clarity; once I start following them, I start comparing myself to others, whether they are following the rules or not, and if not, I am better than them and this pushes me off to the quicksand of my ego."

"So how do you think you can achieve the Supreme Being?" The elderly man asks her.

"The Supreme Being is not a goal to be achieved. I think the ultimate power is an experience. It's a state we can be in, and it can't necessarily to be felt just by following some rules," the girl is dominating their senses now. "And what we can do best to feel God is to be appreciative of what we see around us as God's creation. Be thankful for Its blessings. Or simply don't believe that It even exists! This will force It to reveal Itself."

"By the way what is the relativity here? God is there because of us, or we are here because of God?"

"I have no answer to that question," the elderly man confesses.

"Then what does God do for us? Why is It here in the very first place?" She shoots another one.

"No idea!! God is here because it is just inevitable; because It has no limits so it has to be everywhere, just like air or light," the elderly man tries to conclude the discussion and accept his defeat.

"You resolved your own dilemma, if It is everywhere, we just need to look at It with the right sense, not just by following few rules," the girl claims.

"Regarding your question about who is the cause of existence for whom: God and we are not separate; God is there because of us and we are here because of God. Neither can exist without the other; actually, God and we are one and same. It is just the realization required to merge into It. If we are two different entities then it's a complete failure of Singularity because apart from God, it's humans who have power to think and if we two, I mean, God and us think differently, then it will become a tussle of power between It and us, we would have duality," the Priest weighs in his point of view.

It is mesmerizing to see how someone who was a mentor until a few moments ago is now talking like a disciple.

"Where are you passengers going?" The elderly man changes the topic, which is an assurance that no one is going to die on the boat.

"Kolkata," Bhaijan answers.

"Is she really *the* B-Cube?"

"Yes, I am *the* one," the girl answers.

"Do you know that you killed a gangster last night? You are also being blamed for all of these riots which are happening in Eastern India since you escaped from the brothel in Banaras," the elderly man becomes a bit serious.

"We have lost hundreds of Muslim brothers and sisters since the riots have started; I am sure there will a similar count on the other side as well. Had we not had this discussion, I would have killed you by now and your head would have been served on a platter to your pimps to stop this nonsense," the elderly man replies while fixing his skullcap. "I can take you guys safely to Kolkata but there is no guarantee that you will survive in the city until you reach the consulate. My advice is: go to Dhaka; you don't have to do much, just follow the river and I can volunteer to take you there."

"My boat is a bit more stable for rough currents, so let's change boats; I can help you to go up to Sundarban."

"OK, but how will you come back from there?" The girl replies before Bhaijan and the Priest can.

"You just explained that the second pillar of Islam is to give, which is the most important one after the ultimate confession, and it doesn't need to be practiced. It is a pure intention which anyone can have; I am just trying to follow that," the elderly man replies.

"Donation or the intention of giving is one of the biggest prayers to God. It includes even forgiveness in it. Forgiving people for whatever they have done is the highest level of awareness of the Supreme," the Priest adds to his point.

"Unfortunately, people forget to forgive nowadays; they do give sometimes, but with expectation. And, forgiving by default doesn't come with any expectations so it rarely fits into their scope," Bhaijan says sarcastically.

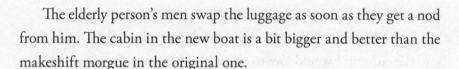

The elderly person's men swap the luggage as soon as they get a nod from him. The cabin in the new boat is a bit bigger and better than the makeshift morgue in the original one.

Meanwhile, the conversation continues:

"That's very true, some of us have simply taken the onus of being a protector on behalf of God, and now we think forgiving is It's duty. Ours is just to give tit-for-tat; an eye for an eye. If someone gives hatred, we give double of it in return," The elderly man says while they embark on their journey. There is a guide in the boat now.

The caravan is moving again. There is fire still burning on both the riverbanks; at some places house and huts are on fire while flames from funeral pyres are leaping to the sky from other sites. However, there is a special composure prevailing on the boat.

Some warm food and tea is served by elderly man to the passengers. The elderly person is standing at the front of the boat and his influence in the area is evident by the attention his boat is getting from the passing by vessels. Police, criminals, anglers etc., all are showing their respect to him.

"So, where were we?" Bhaijan asks in order to continue their earlier conversation.

"The obstacles of Duality in achieving the Singularity, that's what you were talking about," the girl replies.

"Aha! You have brought the conversation right back to where we had left it," the Priest replies.

"For the very first time in my life I have been thinking of something else," the girl is talking to herself while looking at the river.

"We were discussing," the Priest tries to engage the elderly man, but he stops him.

"No, please don't! Let's not bring in history, but allow me to dive into the current; I would love to observe and listen right where it is. Let me be a child entering in your already evolved discussion and interpret it my way," the elderly man finishes his request with beaming eyes.

"By the way, the most important thing at this moment is to teach Breach how to catch fish. This is one of the most prominent areas, where you get fresh water dolphins, and they are really good to practice on, just in case we end up in ocean with whales," Bhaijan states while laughing.

This time he pricks on Breach's face with needle to make it bleed, and then opens her mouth to stick a bone and some flesh in it. Breach eats the flesh. Bhaijan again puts in some more, and continues to do so until Breach's stomach is full. Now, Bhaijan puts in the last bite and throws her in the water.

Breach struggles a little in water, but then finds some dolphins circling around her. Breach has her mouth open and the piece of flesh is clearly visible. A dolphin tries to sneak into it and that is when Breach's hunting skills come out! Breach catches the fish in her mouth and swims towards the boat.

Bhaijan, observing the hunting, pulls the game and prey back on the boat.

"That was amazing; I have never seen a dog become an expert in just two rounds. Breach is brilliant!"

"Do you know why the fish got trapped so easily? And, why a man cannot catch a fish so easily when he has the brain and muscles to use?" The Priest asks.

"Why?" The girl is curious to know.

"Because no animal in this world trusts human beings; they consider humans their biggest enemy; from the lion in a jungle to fish in the ocean, they can rely on their hunters but not on humans. This is how we have made ourselves by continuous betrayal and cruelty against living beings, ever since we stood up on our two feet," the Priest replies.

"So, what is duality, and how can I justify when I am better than anyone else? Let's talk about that," the girl asks them earnestly.

"May be some other time, we already had a lot of in-depth chat. Let's talk about something else," Bhaijan pleads to avoid overdose of Philosophy.

The elderly man is watching them talking, and at the same time, he is keeping an eye around the boat. Every passing vessel is under his surveillance.

"OK, let's talk about you," the Priest says to the girl. "What are you up to in your life? Where exactly are you from in the USA?"

"Well, it's not a long story but definitely a partially blind one," the girl says. "I am not sure if this is the right time to talk about it."

The Priest smiles at her because no one else knows that she is actually partially blind.

"Why don't we play a simple game then?" The elderly man wants to engage in the conversation.

"What type of game?" Bhaijan enquires.

"It's a game of singularity: maybe we will get the answers about the issues of it, or perhaps even discover the need of the duality to achieve the singularity by the time game reaches its climax," the elderly man answers.

"Please elaborate," the girl seems intrigued.

It's already six in the evening, the river stream is getting darker and the moisture, after hanging out in the air for the whole day is returning to its home – the water. The girl is struggling to look around now, but as she is accustomed to such situations, she is easily able to pretend to be a normal girl. Bhaijan is busy skinning the fresh fish that Breach caught. And, the Priest is getting the stove ready for dinner preparation.

"It's a game called Truth," the elderly man explains, "We all know the maturity and beliefs of one another, and above all, we believe in one single God – The Supreme Unknown.

The game is as follows:

We all will tell one tangible and true experience of our life to the rest of the group, and subsequently, define how it correlates with our true goal of life.

Once a person shares his or her experience, the next person must connect the dots to one of his life's experiences and the goal that may correlate with the first person's goal. Remember there are only divine coincidences in this world, all of which have equally divine reasons to occur. The fact that we five living beings are on this boat, it must be for some reason, some common goal.

With this game, we complete the correlation of coincidences for one person.

We will then continue until there is just one person left with final goal and the others are just supporting it. This in no way defines that one person is superior to others but we all as part of super-soul has common path to reach the absolute."

"And how does it help in defining the need of duality and the ultimate singularity of God?" The girl is very excited to play.

"Hmm, so you want to be the first person to start the game?" The elderly man chuckles.

"Why should I?" She opposes hesitantly.

"Well, you are the most curious, as well as the youngest amongst us passengers, and above all you are so far from your home, so it may be that the Almighty has some bigger plan for you," The elderly man clarifies his choice. "And not to worry, you can refuse the offer. The game has already started anyway." He goes and sits on his chair.

"If you start, it will demonstrate how focused you are on your goal and if you don't, then duality is playing on your behalf," he explains further.

"How does duality come into it?" She is still not confident.

"Your confusion to say 'yes or no', and procrastinating from the inevitable, are nothing but duality," the elderly man is master of himself. "Take your time. I would suggest that we remain quiet for tonight and resume the conversation in the morning. By that time, I'm certain we will have someone amongst us ready to volunteer. It will give us enough time to introspect our goals and experiences. Also, you will experience what a fantastic beast silence is."

———————————◆◆◆◆◆◆———————————

Everyone except the girl nod his head in approval of the idea. The game is on!

The elderly man and Bhaijan go inside the cabin to perform their evening Namaaz. The Priest gets busy with the cooking; the girl gets busy at the helm while her half-blind stare is focused on the dark horizon along the river's stream.

A deafening and eternal silence prevails on the boat. Night has fallen on the river; traffic on the water has receded; there are hardly any dolphins diving around in the water now.

The passengers on the boat are within their own thoughts; lost not only in their personal past to scavenge the experience to share the following day, but also struggling to pull out of their future – the goals of their lives. Their tussle with themselves is indicative of the fact that their routine and fight with the world hardly has had any significance or specific purpose. Until now, they never sat in silence to reflect and think about the actual purpose of their life.

They have been, just like the rest of us; fighting a daily battle to survive, but for what, only to die one day? Just to lose the inevitable war when it's time comes?

All of them eat their dinner, with the Priest preferring to have vegetables and the others choosing fish.

Once dinner is over, the passengers are sitting around a small fire pit on the boat. The boat is passing by small villages where different types of religious and folk songs are being played as part of the community chores. Although these songs are thousands of years old, none of them are in praise of God; they are simple messages to live a purposeful life.

The elderly man goes to sleep first, followed by Bhaijan while girl continues the sailing.

The Priest asks the girl to stop the boat. He takes a deep dive into the river, and swims around before coming back on the boat. He is shivering due to the coldness of the water at that time of the night. He changes his clothes and this time gives a white sari to the girl.

It is prayer time for Aghori.

The girl, understanding his intention, also dives in the water, takes a quick dip and returns to the boat.

It is an interesting situation; the same people who were behaving like enemies, have gotten together to embark on an unknown journey. On top of that, one of them proposes to follow a particular way of living for a few hours, and even though it is one of the toughest and most inconvenient ways for a human being to be, the others just follow, without questioning. This is possible only because one critical element of mortality is missing amongst the passengers – expectation.

The girl gets ready in the sari, which is sticking to her wet body.

Bhaijan comes out of the cabin and takes control of the boat; he is navigating swiftly now.

The Priest requests the girl to sit at a clean place in the corner of the boat. Girl knows what to do. She sits on a small wooden plank which is lying there as a lifeguarding raft in the corner. The Priest performs his prayers. He puts colors on her forehead and decorates her with some stale flowers.

The girl is slowly falling into her reality – an illusion to the physical world. Once again she is seeing things clearly. The Priest is chanting his mantras quietly. He then stands up, dances around the girl, and feeds her some sweets. This time she can taste as she has not be spellbound by mysterious liquid.

By now, the girl's eyes have rolled upwards. Her tongue is hanging out of her mouth. Her hair is open and flowing in the wind.

Bhaijan, at the helm of the boat, is busy in his own world, staring at the unknown in the darkness. His only guiding factor is the faded river stream, which itself is tired after a whole day of hardship, but, it is still doing its duty. It seems as if the Ganga knows her goal and she is continuously treading to attain it.

The Priest is tired of dancing by now. He slowly moves towards the girl. He touches her feet and then sits in her small lap.

The girl is still in the same posture. The Priest slowly lies down in her lap and puts his face inside her sari, and his mouth to her breasts. The transparent sari is not hiding anything but still nothing is apparently clear. The Priest, who is wearing just a small bath towel, now lays flat on her lap and it is very clear to see that even though the Priest is sucking at the girl's nipple, this action doesn't have any arousing reaction on his body; the same is the case for the girl as well. To Bhaijan, it looks like a mother feeding her baby.

The Priest goes to sleep on the girl's lap, who is now normal but still staring at the sky. She plays with the Priest's hair like a mother plays with her baby's hair.

She helps to put the Priest to bed and then changes her clothes.

Bhaijan is continuing to sail while the girl sits by the fire stove and cruises the infinite sky in her mind.

Distant music can still be heard as the boat starts to pick up more speed.

———————— ✦✦✦✦✦ ————————

It is early in the morning. The birds are singing their morning chorus with the water revealing the freshness of the new day. The boat stops with a jolt, strong enough to wake up the sleeping passengers.

Bhaijan, the girl and the Priest come out of the cabin to discover that the boat is nearby the riverbank. The elderly man is buying some food items from a local farmer in another boat. Everyone is curious to see whether he is speaking to that person.

Human behavior can be so strange!! Just a few hours earlier, they were all strangers, but once the elderly man joined them on their journey, it didn't take much time for them to follow his guidelines. Now in even lesser time than that, they are once again doubting that he is in the process of breaking his promise to each of the passengers.

The elderly man returns to the boat and serves tea and breakfast to all of them. It is now that they realize that he was just buying breakfast and tea for them. However, since they have seeds of doubt sown in their mind, they are reluctant to eat and drink anything bought by him.

"Did you speak to him?" The girl is about to ask the elderly man this question, but he stops her from breaking the silence.

"No," is the elderly man's reply by the shaking of his head. He notices the clouds of doubts in the others' mind. He goes to each of them and takes a sip of tea from their cup to clear the air.

The tension on the boat melts with those sips of assurance. Silent music is being played by the wind. And the morning dance performed by the sunlight shining on the water surface as seen at this moment and at this place in time, will never be repeated again in this universe. The morning mist is again going back to the unknown in the sky, only to return later in the evening.

"So now, that silence has to be broken, here we are, back in the game. Should we start?" The elderly man asks without wasting time, "I thank all of you for following my request. May you speak on Allah's behalf and enlighten us about the importance of being not only truthful but also of what our true goal is in this precious opportunity – Life."

"Amen," Bhaijan and the girl nod their head in approval.

"Let's take fifteen minutes to get ready. There is no restriction on speaking now, but the more we remain silent, the more we will remain focused on our experience and goal," the elderly man recommends. "We already had a small distraction of mistrust this morning."

His last statement is followed by the lowering of heads of the passengers; perhaps as a confession of the fact, and the shame accompanying it.

Again, the Priest takes off his clothes and takes a plunge in the river. When he comes back on the boat, he gets ready in one of his best dresses, which is nothing but an old yellow satin rob; he puts on his horizontal three-liner white color mark called a 'Tripund', with a red dot in the middle on his forehead.

He lights some incense sticks and fixes them in the corner of the boat, where he recited his prayers last night.

Bhaijan and the elderly man go for their Namaaz after the Priest takes over control of navigating. He continues to mumble some chants. He does not look within himself as usual.

Slowly, his mumblings transition to very clear chants, and subsequently much louder shouts.

He is praising his deity as the boat sails by a tall lord Shiva statue on the riverbank. The Priest's stare towards the statue is very intense and filled with the determination of a child who is staring at his parents in an attempt to earn a sweet. He keeps on turning his head as the boat passes the statue.

Suddenly he changes his mind and steers the boat with a complete U-turn towards the idol, and then slows it down. It has been almost twelve hours since the boat has been sailing without any proper stops.

He docks the boat at the statue site; some fires are burning but there is no one nearby them. The scene looks familiar to the girl, but she is not able to recall, where she has seen such fires before.

He picks up his skull bowl and jumps out of the boat towards the bank. He collects some wildflowers from the nearby bushes as he approaches the Shiva statue, and places those flowers as offerings at Shiva's feet. He lies flat on his stomach with his full body stretched out, and his hands and head at Shiva's feet.

He stands up after almost an entire minute, and goes to the river with his skull bowl in his hands. He fills the bowl with water from the Ganga, and drinks it as it spills from the sides of his mouth. After drinking, he once again takes a dip in the water. His recently applied Aghori makeup has washed away now. Completely soaked in water, he heads straight towards one of the extinguished fires, where hot coal pieces are still glowing amber. He collects some of the hot ash from that pit.

There are some stone like objects mixed with coal in the fire. Once the Priest picks up the bowl, full of ash, the girl in the boat realizes that the place is nothing but a cremation ground, and the fire pits are nothing but funeral pyres. The stones in the bowl are nothing but bones. Someone has just turned up as ashes while embarking on a new journey.

The Priest scavenges through the pits before finalizing one as his preference. He collects a lot of fine and hot ash from that pit in his half-filled skull bowl and pours it over his head. He smears the ash all over his still-wet body. He looks like an overly made up woman now, with his body covered with ashes from head to toe. You can see red fire flakes stuck in the ashes on his body, combined with his red eyes, and some black hair of his beard peeking out from the remaining painted ones. He goes back to Shiva's statue once again and prostrates flat at its feet.

After finishing his ritual, he re-joins the passengers on the boat.

Bhaijan and the elderly man also come out of the cabin. Their faces look tired, but glowing with a mysterious aura. Someone is praying to dead; some to deadly while some are afraid of the death!

Bhaijan takes over the helm of the boat and starts sailing it.

"Are we ready?" The girl asks them while still staring at the Priest's makeup.

"Ladies first," the Priest literally shouts out casually with his yellowish teeth beaming in an ear-to-ear smile.

"OK, as you say and insist lovingly.

I have tried a lot to think of an amazing experience in my life, but cannot find one as amazing as I have encountered just a few moments ago! However, I do have a very horrible chain of experiences that forced me to define the goal of my life. In fact, these very experiences defined me to be what I am today. I think the goal of my life is a very violent one, full of vengeance, and it doesn't fit in any of the schools of thought of religion or philosophy, still, I think my only reason to remain in this world is to achieve this particular goal; doesn't matter if it is wrong or even a sin. It also doesn't matter if I even have to shun every single comfort and luxury of this world to achieve my goal," she pauses to look at the audience for their interest in her life-story.

"Please continue. We will always be listening, and above all, when someone is not listening or understanding what you are trying to say, don't get disheartened; it either means that people are not eligible to listen to you, or you are communicating directly with The Ultimate One – The Supreme," the elderly man assures her to continue speaking without stopping to gauge their reaction.

Joan's eyes are shut; she is sitting with Breach by her side. Sunrays are fully bright now and falling straight on her face. She immediately dives into a deep dream.

"My experience goes as…" as Joan starts unravelling, so do the tears from her eyes.

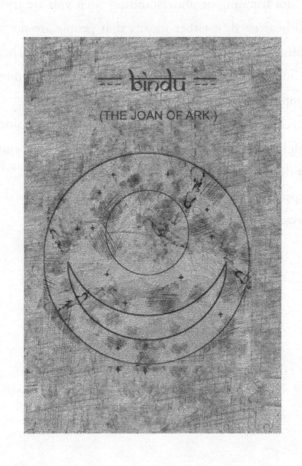

= bindu =

(THE JOAN OF ARK)

--- BINDU ---

THE JOAN OF ARK

"Somewhere deep in my heart, I still cherish those beautiful days when we had moved to a small cabin in the deep woods of Pennsylvania, USA," the girl literally transfers to her home while in her imagination, "I still remember those purposeless days, when I used to spend the whole morning watching birds and enjoying their musical chirping.

Nights were spent listening to different types of songs and drumbeats by beers and wolves.

Somebody once said: good times fly by with ignorance, but difficult times test you each and every moment.

Such was my life. Almost two months had flown by, with me doing absolutely nothing. I was just spending time and enjoying the wildlife without any efforts. Maybe I wanted to be one with nature during that time.

People forgot to give the reason of why good time flies by: it does, because you are not learning anything, you are not experiencing anything deep during those times. You become so extroverted and consumed in savoring the goodness.

However, when we go through a difficult time, we are aware of every moment of it. We are on a steep learning curve. We are so cautious and calculated in our moves that we know those steps clearly. In short, we have an in-depth experience because we are putting our efforts to pull things that are not going our way; and these types of lessons become unforgettable for us. They are like nails hammered deep inside us. It is a period when we live the most and learn the most."

I, a partially blind teenage girl (who can see blurred watery images during the brightest time of a sunny day), whose world revolved around two people: her father, Jesus and twin brother Andrew, as well as her dog Breach. My happy family's fate turned dramatically and drastically unfortunate when Andrew became a drug peddler after our mother's death. Our father, a professor of Psychology, tried his best to help Andrew mend his ways, but that turned out to be fatal for his small family.

He sacrificed his career by retiring early, and moving to a secluded cabin in the woods of Pennsylvania. Dad thought it would help Andrew's rehabilitation to be in such a serene location right after he was released from jail after serving his prison term. But, it didn't work. Andrew left us at the first opportunity that came along. My father broke down and could never think of coming out of those woods, hoping that Andrew would come back to us one day.

And he did, Andrew, who had suddenly disappeared a few months before, returned home one day! He lived with us for quite some time with very optimistic signs of recovering from his past. What we did not know was that he was actually hiding from the cops after a horrific gang war in Buffalo city.

One day my dad caught him sniffing cocaine. A father's scolding to his young son, quickly converted to an argument between a fuming dad and a criminal son. Subsequently it unfolded into a dispute between two angry men and that ended in a fatal fight between two violent animals.

Andrew, not in the fit of rage, but calmly and intentionally, killed our dad. With my partial visibility and senses, I witnessed the slow and painful final moments of my father's life. Those moments were really bad, but certainly not the worst thing that happened to me on that fateful day.

Andrew did not stop after killing our dad. He crossed the limits of morality and cruelty beyond imagination when he raped me, multiple times for next three days. For the first couple of times I thought he was under the influence of drugs, and will realize his grave mistakes once he regained his senses, but I was wrong. I still remember every second of that day, but none of the fresh mornings that I spent with the birds. He left me half-alive in the woods, to be eaten by bears and wolves.

His intentions were clear when he left the doors open along with a trail of blood in the woods to attract animals. But…. I survived the trauma, with the help of my dog – Breach.

◆◆◆◆◆

I was unconscious for many days; I do not even know for how long, as I lost count for those days of my life. I was lying alongside with the cold and mutilated body of my beloved father in the open cabin. Somehow, one day, I opened my eyes and could see sunshine after all this. I survived! I remained alive to embark on the journey of my life to achieve only one goal, and that is to find and kill my own brother, Andrew.

I was unable to move and see clearly but slowly recovered from my physiological injuries. It took me days to be able to just stand up and move around the house. I could not even close the doors to keep the cabin a bit warm until I regained some physical energy. Breach was the one who licked my numerous open wounds and kept them clean.

During those initial moments after recovery, I stumbled upon the dead bodies of some wolves and bear cubs'. The condition of the cabin floor was clearly indicative of the violent battles Breach had gone through to keep me alive. There were carcasses of at least fifty wolves and many young bear cubs, scattered in the main hall. They say: fortune favors the brave, but for me it was – fortune just pities me – my stars not only begged for life from my death during that period, but also paved the way to meet you people. I was able to preserve a lot of meat for the coming months.

I was healing physically with time, but I made sure that I did not lose the psychological wounds.

With a clear objective in my mind, I started training myself to overcome my weaknesses; I trained to make myself strong. I practiced following Breach wherever she would go. One of the toughest things in the world is to listen to the footsteps of a dog and that is what I made myself an expert at. I started seeing through those paw-steps. I climbed mountains and trees. I starved myself for days so that I could get my breasts down to look like man's chest. I went to the extreme extent of even cutting the remaining flesh around my breasts to make them as flat as I can. The cross signs on my chest are results of from those attempts only.

I was not making myself stronger than males in society to fight them and prove myself superior, but rather, I was developing my strength to be durable enough to bear the pain given by the world.

I was not on a mission to prove myself, but I was on a journey to experience the pain to achieve my goal.

It is only until a certain day that a person will think of all the luxuries and comforts and stresses and any other damn excuse in this world. It is until this certain day that he or she will consider that they are living just to satisfy their five senses. But, when the *real* time comes, with the *real* goal of life revealed in front of them, every other thing in the life: family, friends, foes, bread and butter, wine and whines, simply becomes secondary.

This is the actual realization of the purpose of human life.

This was what was transpiring in my life at that moment. I had nothing left in my mind, except the burning fire and desire to achieve my goal. That goal is to kill Andrew – my brother at any cost.

My first challenge was to find where Andrew would be, his whereabouts. I had nothing, no clue, and no lead.

It was first time since I went inside the woods that I came out of the jungle. I thought I would be received by the nicest of the people in the world, only to find one police officer, who helped me for a 'favor' in locating my way back to the cabin, where my father's dead body was lying, rotting.

I, who had just come out of the first ever penetration in her life, and that too as a rape by my own brother, learnt in a very hard way, the commodity I had in my possession to sell in the 'more-brutal-than-the-jungle civilized world'. The laws of the jungle are challenging, but the anarchy of the civilized jungle is unpardonable. You make one choice against it, you expose one weakness to it and it will usurp you slowly and painfully. It is a market – you are always either selling something, or buying something. Sometimes you are selling your skills, sometimes your body, and sometimes even your own spirit.

The officer, as part of such a 'socialized world', also raped me multiple times but in return, he provided me details about Andrew; he sold his spirit for two minutes of forced pleasure. As per him, Andrew was not traceable by the cops. He was already on the FBI's most wanted list. Most probably, he had left the country. He also told me that I should head east if I wanted to have even a one percent chance of seeing him again. Once I had this useless information about Andrew, I made the officer pay the ultimate price for exploiting my weakness.

Before hunting fishes, Breach used to hunt giant bears very well.

I moved from one challenge to the next in my quest to find Andrew, who could be anywhere in this world. My first task was to be a bit more muscular so that my 'clients' simply pay me and move along without inflicting any more psychological pain on me. I knew I could bear the pain but this was not sufficient to progress.

Once I was ready to move to next step, I found a pleasant surprise in my life – Love – It was actually a distraction from my path. My roommate in the one room apartment in New York that I rented; started approaching me. And even I liked his warm presence around me. Although I could not see him properly, I was very fond of his voice and his shady figure whenever he was home.

The ephemeral dream backfired, when I got in bed with him, with the hope of having some joy of love. I found myself in the middle of a human traffickers' gang from Mexico, who kidnapped me and took me to an unknown place for 'business'. I always wonder about the value of humanity, and the invaluable-ness of speechless animals with no demands. Breach followed me wherever I went or dwarfed by my own destiny. It has been such a mysterious bond between the two of us, that even all the adversaries I met, during my journey until today, ignored

Breach as some useless body part of mine, which is required to sell my useful two inches…"

"After months of forced travels; sometimes in containers; sometimes in carton boxes stuffed like a loaf of meat; after numerous sexual exploitations and tortures – I met Aghori, only to know that now I am here, in India, with you guys on a journey." The girl completes her story with tears in her eyes.

= vishuddha =

(THE PASSENGERS)

--- VISHUDDHA ---
(THE PASSENGERS)

Her life has shaken everyone. They are feeling the guilt of being a man, sitting in front of a woman, who is asking them to explain why men are the way they are. Nature has given them the power to save, not the arrogance to exploit. They are so absorbed in her experience that the pain she has gone through is clearly reflected on their faces.

The river span has grown wider now. There are many more arteries merging and Ganga has become a confluence of many streams; including waste from factories, towns and fields, but the purity of the name and the faith of people is still intact. The banks passing by are still full of pilgrims. They are trying to heal their souls, and clean their hearts with the holy water of Ganga.

"Tormenting is you experience, and vengeance is your goal," the elderly summarizes.

"I won't put a noun, or an adjective for my experience and goal here," girl counters. "Because I am not marketing it – I have lived through the experience and I am living for my goal, that's it."

The Priest is crying aloud now; he is blank and staring in the sky, while shouting at the unknown in a language only known to him perhaps. The girl hugs him to assuage his pain. She knows the pain of feeling guilty is far worse than the pain of being a victim.

"I was part of the Great Revolution!" The elderly man starts talking about his experience as soon as there is some peace on the boat.

"Being from Afghanistan, I was tasked to supply opium and marijuana to the Army. The common mass of my new country had nothing to do with politics and international relationships; all they wanted to do was live their life in their own way."

He stands on the side of the boat smoking his Hookah and staring at the growing darkness as it emerges downstream. The east has the privilege to see the first sunrays at the dawn, but at the same time, it also bears the burden of facing the dark earlier than the west does.

"I thought I was helping Islam grow; I thought, the more countries that are Islamic, the more peaceful this world be. For me Islam was Islam: one unified world of peaceful scholars and believers. However, I was wrong!

I had a different status in Afghanistan compared to what I had in the new country.

For the majority of Afghanis, who are Sunnis, I was a 'Hashashoon', which means from a gang of betrayers who have given the word 'assassin' to the English dictionary. Whereas, for my neighbors, who are mostly Shite; I was the descendent of the martyrs who had laid down their life for Imam Husain, the beloved grandson of our Holy Paigamber."

＋◆◆◆◆＋

"So, as my story goes, just after the revolution, I was not able to move from this place, due to its bitter rivalry with the western world.

For my unknown bosses, their purpose of doping the common masses and steering them towards religious vigor had been extremely successful. People, who used to think earlier, had now become like cattle.

Their purpose and struggle was just to show off how religious they are; the length of their beard became matter of the pride, instead of the adjectives in their names.

Political agents and religious leaders once again won the battle and started to work around what was selfishly best for them.

Women started covering themselves, so that they do not become the reason of men's deviation from their seemingly religious duties. The opposite happened, however. Men were now becoming excited to see even the toes of a woman – a Supply and Demand law came into effect there.

I, being a rationally religious person, started to feel suffocated by this new culture, but I had nothing to worry about. What I had considered my religious duty previously: to supply pleasure medicines to the masses had become my full-fledged profession by now. Earlier people felt enticed to use it; now they were addicted to it, and I could sell the opium at my defined prices.

I became part of the most influential coterie of businesspeople, religious leaders and politicians, who were even beyond Allah in the country.

During all of this personal economic progression, I was struggling to understand – what the meaning of life is, who Allah is? I could experience It but not see It. This introspection became more vociferous when I became part of the warriors who were fighting against the Sunnis.

◆◆◆◆◆◆

Muslims, in spite of being world conquerors, were struggling to hold one piece of land.

Actually, we stopped remaining at peace immediately after the departure of the Holy Prophet Mohammad, peace be upon him. This perhaps needs some introspection.

Anyway, the bitterness sown amongst the allied Shite countries was creating a new twist there. People started to become very interested in having western women as sex slaves. No matter what the Quran actually says, their mullahs twisted facts and gave them permission through the declaration of fatwas, to follow such ridiculous traditions.

It is not mentioned anywhere in the Quran, to denigrate women. In fact, Paigamber Mohammad himself has said – heaven resides beneath our mother's feet. According to him, a mother is next to Allah itself.

Nevertheless, the Mullahs did not see the world from the same perspective as Mohammad did. They provided 'guidelines'. And they did so according to their knowledge, and inclination towards this world. They also wanted to be powerful; they wanted people to follow them, and this desire, to be powerful and to be followed, brought such fatwas. They acquired a weapon of Mass destruction called Qafir – the apostate.

It is true that the Quran is one of the most revered and unchanged scripts revealed by God himself, but now, it is one of the most misinterpreted, and badly represented philosophies in world. No one can deny this. Every devout Muslim who insists – Islam is the religion of peace; faces ridicule from others.

People opened schools to teach Quran and provide interpretations according to the funding provided by the power centers. These centers are shrewd enough not to write their own versions, and to just create confusion amongst the masses – the way the church did in Christianity or the way Seers did in Hinduism. They cleverly misinterpreted Divine text and presented it to the innocents.

This new misadventure of keeping Western or 'Qafir' women as slaves became a big boom business.

I was personally against it, but it came down to my life. In spite of being seen as the devoted, five times a day praying person that I am, I was declared an American agent. I was forcefully pushed into this business. I still don't know if it's not only God that is invisible or the demon is also the same, because I couldn't find any face that was forcing me to do such dastardly acts.

My skills of navigating through international waters and my connection with African mafias proved to be lucrative to these vultures.

I was tasked to run the human trafficking ring from Mexico, and bring western girls to be sold to the riches in the region. The business provided huge money for my gangs, but it made me poor from the inside.

Slowly, I became part of this new culture of slavery. I myself became a slave of the Mullahs, as soon as I started fulfilling their demands.

It continued until the day I heard about a mysterious witch in one of my shipments. I learnt that there is a satanic girl in this new consignment from Mexico, and that she is a black magician who travels with a black dog.

The arrogance within a man to conquer a woman more powerful than himself, brought to surface a wild storm in me.

I decided to take this witch in my servitude. She was indeed a satanic black magician. Her presence was enough to bring bad omens in to my life. She was the only one, apart from me, who survived the storm in the sea on that fateful night.

Somehow, we reached land, and she stayed in my house as a slave. Soon thereafter, I caught my wife having illicit affairs with my servants; my daughter ran away from home with one of her bodyguards; I lost my entire business. The so-called coterie of influences disappeared to thin air overnight. Afghanis started calling me a Shite Muslim- a traitor, and others taunted me for the fact that I am an Afghani. It was fascinating for me to hear their preference of adjectives, just to get rid of me. All the wealth I had collected during the whole revolution fiasco, and afterwards just evaporated from my pocket.

I left, with just a couple of lives with me. One was the only servant who never spoke to me, and the other was her dog. Apart from these two beings, I had one boat and some of the connections I had developed in the deep seas for my rainy days.

Those very Mullahs who authorized me to buy slaves, issued a new Fatwa against me for human trafficking, it is just so awful to see people with power getting away with manipulating perceived truths as per their convenience.

Anyway, as Joan said, those were the times when I learnt about true friends, I was alone against whole world on that day. I embarked upon my journey to an unknown destination. I realized that the purpose of my life was not to sit idle in a jail, but to go to the deep blue sea and find it.

The black magician witch was caught by the police and sentenced to death by stoning, but, then there was the problem of her burial. The scholars decided that the body of this witch must be dumped in the sea. I took this job to beg pardon for myself and promised not to return ever again. I bargained for the Fatwa against me to be revoked. The deal worked out, and so did my confidence that I am headed in the right direction. The path was opening new horizons for me.

I embarked on this final journey, prepared to dump the girl in the water grave on my way to Mumbai where I knew a few people who could help me hide from my enemies.

For the very first time, I desired to sin. I desired to have some intimacy with the girl; by choice, or if required, by force. Just to play with fire and experience it. The fire that destroyed my whole world, I wanted to incinerate it. Anyway, it was clear that she was going to die. But, when I stripped her, I found two crosses etched on the chest of the black witch.

I saw her using a wooden pestle for self-humiliation and that she had no resistance whatsoever towards any person having sex with her. In fact, she wanted men to try the cruelest ways of hurting her soul. She had become a sadist, and I felt miserable about her attitude towards her own dignity. Finally, I gave up the idea of further hurting her, or even killing her. I realized that I was not facing a destroyer but a destroyed one.

I never dared to touch her, not because of her notoriety of being a witch, but because my conscience did not allow me to do so. Respect for women, empathy for the suppressed, these values stopped me from satisfying my ego.

However, fate had something else written for both of us. Our boat was struck by a storm in the Arabian Sea and it was completely wrecked. Rather than helping each other, the girl had some other plans. She used the same material: the heavy rocks, coffin and ropes that I had brought to bury her in the ocean, to tie me up and leave me to drown and become food for the fish. I was in the middle of nowhere, left to think about Allah and the purpose of life. And to figure out how to come out of the situation I found myself in; or perhaps just to wait for my death.

I was inside the floating coffin without water or food, for almost a week, with the only ray of hope peeking from a small crack at the lid of the coffin. She hadn't put enough weight on the coffin, so that I could have the agonizing and slow meeting with my truth – Death.

———————— ✦✦✦✦✦ ————————

Sea burial coffins are generally airtight at base, so that the body remains intact for a while. Maybe Allah inspired our predecessors to make them airtight so that I could save myself on that fateful day. This is what we call calculated moves of the Great Almighty. 'It' is not visible to anyone but always thinks about us. It even encourages people to make calculated mistakes, like the fissure in the lid of my coffin.

I did not have an apocalypse on that day; my destiny had something else in mind, in spite of losing everything that I had, except my breath; I was curious to know who the black witch was. Is there anything I can do for her?

I became 'Poshida' – invisible – inside the coffin. It was quite an experience! I was floating around the coffin. I could see at a distance; sometimes, ships passed by what I thought was my final bed; they could not see me, but I could see them. I was trying to talk to them and explain that whatever they were doing is not what they are supposed to do. I was not pleading to them to open the coffin because that hardly mattered to me anymore.

I screamed at them but they could not hear me. Finally, there came the ultimate moment of my life. One day I saw the girl had returned. She could see me sitting on top of my coffin. She dragged my coffin until it reached the shoreline and then, she disappeared in to thin air. She didn't say a word during this rescue but her eyes were clear: "Wait for me; I will need you to return this favor."

Even though, I was Poshida for the world, I had clearly encountered a soul much more motivated and clear about her goal than I was about mine. In fact, *she* became my goal. For the very first time I saw and experienced God.

◆◆◆◆◆

Tides took me to the shore, and for the first time I felt the solid base beneath my coffin. Now the coffin was like my mother's womb to me. I was still confined inside the box, yet happy to know that I am going to live. It was still dark inside, but the rays of hope had reinvigorated my spirit. This was how I felt in a situation where my physical strength hardly mattered, because, I was so elevated spiritually that I could have flew above the earth.

A Good Samaritan broke my coffin in the hope of finding a few fish to feed his family. Actually, that is the only thing we need in life, everything else is just what we want, or perhaps, what we greed for.

Disheartened by the fact that it was not fish but an almost dead human being, he left me there but with the coffin open. I was not even able to move out of the boundary of death and birth. What others saw from the outside was a coffin, but from the inside, I was taking rebirth in this world.

The good old man returned after a while with some fresh water and a loaf of bread. It reminded me – that our soul doesn't even need food; its actual source of energy is the good work its bearer does. The old man was wary of me, but beaming with optimism that I have survived the infinite.

I recovered quickly with the blessings of the old man. I had always been afraid of unknown enemies. My savior won the prize of life when I connected him with a well-routed smuggling racket. I told him about my personal history, as well as about the only fear that I had in my mind. He helped me move to this hinterland of India – Bihar. His growing influence and our mutual respect to and for each other brought me fame and power in this part of the world.

I was still not able to be at peace because the girl was haunting me in my dreams, her dog was mauling me every night, and she had just one demand – I owe her a life. I owe her at least some guidance to help her achieve her goal. It is required because it is the goal of my life. Just like building an airtight coffin was the goal in life of numerous undertakers and Mullahs, so that it could help me in achieving my goal.

And now I am in the final stage of achieving my goal as I take Joan to her destination."

◆ ◆◆◆◆ ◆

"What??" Bhaijan and the Priest scream together.

"It's been almost 5 years now," the elderly man replies with very calm expressions.

"Tell me one thing: why didn't you kill me before dumping me in the coffin? You had enough strength to do that," the elderly man asks Joan.

"I don't know, maybe I wanted you to be safe so that one day you could save me; maybe the so called Adrushya Guru –The Poshida One – instigated me to let you be where you are; maybe it has some long-term plan that is becoming clearer now."

"But one thing was sure; I had both hatred and respect for you at that time, if it really was actually *you* who had taken me as slave.

Hatred, because you respected me; you did not hurt me the way I was being hurt by other males. This seemed like abnormal behavior to me, and it weakened my commitment to abhor all men in this world.

And respect, because of the same reasons; that there are human beings in this world who *do* think differently who treat women as equal participants in this created universe."

"But what happened to you after you left?" Bhaijan asks.

"I don't know; my makeshift boat kept sailing without fuel until I was trapped by yet another gang of human traffickers. They took me in their boat and reignited the fire of disgust in me by raping and harassing me on a regular basis. Finally, I was taken to an unknown location, which was Banaras, as I later learnt from you and the Priest," the girl replies to summarize.

It's late in the evening, the sun has set at the back of the boat and moonlight is scattered on the tiny waves of the Ganga's water.

Bhaijan steers the boat to a barren sandy island in the middle of the river.

All the passengers disembark there. Although they are travelling in one of the most comfortable boats available, still the impact of continuous movement and swaying along with the wind and water has changed the inertia of their bodies. Their exhausted footsteps fall erratically on the solid ground.

Bhaijan again preps Breach to go fishing, which is not one of the most interesting things for her to do.

The Priest finds what he always aspires to have for his prayer: a funeral pyre. He walks towards the fire, which is at a bit of a distance from the bank.

The girl prefers to take a quick dip in the water, which is still relatively warm from the daylight.

The elderly man is busy in bringing out items from the kitchen in order to prepare dinner.

There is a prolonged silence all around. All that can occasionally be heard are chants from the priest and squeaks from the bats to break the equilibrium.

The Priest returns with his body smeared with fresh ash and burning wood to light a fire for them. Breach has returned with a fish in her mouth, big enough to serve four. The elderly man has finished chopping vegetables, and Bhaijan has the rice ready to cook.

They try their best to light a fire with the limited wood available, without any success. Finally, a silent consent is reached amongst the passengers to move to funeral pyre and cook dinner on that.

The group moves to the center of the small island and settle down around the cozy experience of life and death. Someone is burning to provide warmth and food to others; maybe that was the goal of that deceased person's life, or perhaps the goal of his or her death.

Nobody is speaking to the outside world, but there is a commotion happening inside the universe. Expressions are missing on their faces but their souls are screaming. Everybody finishes his or her food before going to their sandy beds around the funeral pyre.

Breach is guarding the surroundings; she is even keeping her eye on the boat. Perhaps with the recent cremation that has taken place, the island is relatively safe as no one is courageous enough to come to the island during the night. It is so hard to face the truth of death for all of us.

The elderly man is awakened due to turmoil happening around the dosed off fire. He realizes that some villagers have restrained Bhaijan and the girl. Everyone in the group have their torso shaved and are wearing a small wet towel. It does not take much time to realize that these people are the near and dear ones of the soul whose body was unionized with the five fundamental elements here in the funeral pyre last night.

They are here to collect the ashes and bones of the deceased person to immerse in the Ganga by his or her loved ones.

However, they are angry at a Muslim taking shelter in the warmth of the funeral pyres. The elderly man has escaped their wrath because he was not wearing his skullcap; dressed in jean pants and a kurta with a fully-grown beard and moustache gives him a very different look.

It is amazing to see how a simple change in clothes and appearance can give a different color to your religious beliefs. A short pajama is enough for one to be misunderstood as a terrorist or fanatic. A beard with a clean moustache, which was shaved in order to provide enough breathing space in the sweltering sun, can make you look like a hard-core extremist instead of a devoted seer who didn't have time to shave, as he was busy in self-conversation. This same beard has also protected him from mosquitoes, and the freezing cold. Nevertheless, to hell with religion and science and above all common sense once anger prevails.

The Priest is sitting in a meditative state, looking like a mendicant with fresh human-ash smeared on his body. A seemingly close relative, maybe a son or husband whose duty it was to light-up the fire due to being closest in relation to the deceased, is sobbing with his head on the Priest's lap.

"Yes, I cooked food in this fire, but what does that matter? Fire is the purest of the forms of matter, so why do you think that the funeral is desecrated by the mere touch of a Muslim? Even hell relies upon fire to cure the incurables and purify the impure," Bhaijan addresses the crowd.

People thrash him brutally once again, and Bhaijan bears the latest barrage with a painful smile. They probably do not have any answer to Bhaijan's queries; hence, it suits them better to suppress his voice.

"I have already told you that I can speak to the departed soul and it is more than happy to serve humans irrespective of religion –because it has reached a state where spirits are just spirits – without any boundaries or constraints of beliefs or religion. They themselves are the beliefs; they are omnipresent and filled with equanimity," the Priest tries to interject.

The faith in the eyes of the crowd has changed; not against Bhaijan but now, it is raging against the Priest. A venerable aghori, who has the authority to guide them, has just said something that does not fit their assumptions; it is not the same outcome as they were expecting. The masses are more powerful than the authority of the sole Aghori.

"Aghori Babaji, we understand your love for these people. It looks like you also had some dinner and dance with them last night. We were wondering about the music coming from the island for the whole night. Earlier, we ignored it, thinking that our ancestors are welcoming grandmother into their company. However, now we realized that it was not the music of spirits, but from this Mujra at the funeral. Shame on people like you; who denigrate Sanaatan Dharma. We sacrifice our flesh and bones for you people, just to make sure that you attain the acme of Tantra and help all in society to liberate them. This sacrifice in no way allows you to deviate from the path defined by Shiva," a seemingly religiously erudite individual expresses his detailed but assumed opinion to add fuel to the fire of suspicion that is already burning amongst the crowd.

"And what is the path defined by Shiva, peace be upon him?" The elderly man interjects.

"Who are you?" A person hiding in the crowd asks him. "As an elder you should have told them what is right and what is not." This is the face of falsehood, it has a voice and many faces but certainly no tangibility; it always speaks from behind and hides, as soon as its work is done.

"Ismail," a plain worded response comes from the elderly man. The face, expressions and voice are all clear – Here comes the truth.

"Ohh, he is an imposter Muslim!" Shouts the faceless crowd again. Deceit is scared now, hence it screams at the one and only – the fact.

"EkoVaDwitiyamNasti! Does that make me a Hindu?" The elderly man counters them. "I brought the girl and sailor Bhaijan, to this place last night. Sadhu baba was already sleeping here and did not have any role in what was cooked or eaten here. In fact, he objected to what we were trying to do, and we complied with his concerns. We didn't touch any of the material in the funeral pyre. We just used the heat to keep ourselves warm and cook some food. Actually, we did not even realize that it is a funeral pyre, or else it was Haraam for us to cook there. Islam forbids the burning of a body or even touching the fire that is used to burn bodies. So, the Priest is as pure as the fire, which can convert everything into five basic elements." The elderly is putting the safety of the three lives above his and beyond the truth.

◆ ◆ ◆ ◆ ◆

The people's perception changes again, but one thing is sure, during these conversations, even the person who is grieving the most within the crowd, has forgotten his pain. He is now more interested to know who is at fault to impure the purest of the pure – the Fire.

"So, tell me now, what is my punishment?" The elderly man asks the crowd, "I do not know mantras and chants; I never believed in idols because my God, Allah resides in each one of us; but I do know what is appropriate at this moment. If you are looking for a Barbariek to donate his head here, ask me for it, and I, Ismail, the Muslim, will be happy to repeat history and be one of the numerous occasions where self-sacrifice was required to realize the reality for masses."

Most of the people in the crowd are shocked, except one who sees this as an opportunity to test another's faith.

"Aghori baba, let's assume that you are not at fault, what is your opinion about this? We will obey your judgement but make sure that forgiveness is not an option here, especially for a person from another religion, it cannot be tolerated at any cost," he challenges the Priest to decide with his own imposition on the decision.

The elderly man smiles sarcastically because he can clearly see the shrewd mullah in the garb of a Hindu scholar who wants to use his influence on the religious sentiments of the masses for his own benefits. It is such as risk-free strategy to grow one's clout; if it works then it cements their command on the decision, and if it doesn't work, the decision maker will be blamed, while the mullah or pundit still get their voice heard by the crowd.

"Aghori is not here to judge but to be judged, and to be judged only by Maha-aghori – Shiva!" The Priest is angry now.

He throws a tantrum on the almost dosed fire. But, the bones in the ashes are still very hot and the Priest is dancing on the burning bones. His violent ritual is that of the Tandava – a Dance of apocalypse, performed by Shiva when he decided to destroy the world.

Seeing things getting out of control, Bhaijan frees himself from the people's grip and picks up the skull bowl of Aghori. He fills it with water from a bucket, brought by the people and pours it on the fire. A huge plume of smoke and vapor rises from the ashes and covers the dancing Priest.

The elderly man and girl jump in the fire and bring Aghori out of it. He is still angry and shaking in rage. Although burnt by the fire, the girl ignores her pain and hugs the Priest like a mother trying to persuade her son not to play dangerous games. People are mesmerized by the drama as they witness it unfolding: the sadness, excitement, mystery, anger, frustration, confusion, jealousy, respect and awe, everything is at the deathbed struggling to find an answer for their meaning; the purpose of the religion. Also, some of the deceased person's beloved ones are searching for the mortal bones in the ashes desperately.

"Pundit, be as impartial as your deity is and tell us what should be done here to resolve this issue!" Bhaijan screams at the Priest with a choking throat.

The Priest is a bit calmer now; he sits in a meditation position and closes his eyes. His body is still shaking; his eyes are wet.

It takes him almost an hour to open his eyes, which is an equally eternal time for people, impatient to go home, as well as those who care about the situation that has arisen.

"If the person who has cooked food on the pyre is a true believer in Advaita, then he needs to sacrifice and donate his own flesh, equal to the weight of what he cooked on the pyre."

"What is Advaita?" A person with a clean torso and a big red mark on his forehead asks.

"It is good to ask a question, even if it is a stupid one," the Priest reacts with a rare smile at the question," because it gives you a small window to assess the answerer as well."

The person bows his head in shame and moves back to his place in the crowd.

"Advaita is the belief in a single God – the ultimate singularity – that cannot be seen or heard but felt and experienced in the other-worldly enigma."

"This is what I said earlier: EkoVaDwitiyamNasti," the elderly man says. "It is La-Ilahe-Ill-Allah in Arabic."

"But this rule doesn't fit Muslims!" A cleric amongst the people claims.

"Why not? This fundamental concept existed even before Islam was born. Moreover, it is not the rule of any religion. It is a foundational law of nature. It is the principal of God, who is one and just one. If you think it is different, then you also do not believe in Advaita!" The Priest literally screams his reply. He stands up and fills his human skull with ash and water. "If you do not believe in this rule then you do not believe in the Sanaatan Dharma. Now I stand up to defend my Dharma, let's see who is against it!" He is back in Siva's Tandava form, with one leg crossed in the air and hair openly flying in the wind. His stare with burning red eyes is enough for the argument of the pseudo-faithful to hide behind the doubt of being right or wrong.

"Bhaijan, get a fish similar to the one that was cooked here last night and cut an equal amount of flesh from your body," orders the Priest.

Bhaijan and Breach rush towards the Ganga. The purity of Ganga is still intact. The air of the river is listening to the conversation and has a fish ready at the bank; half-buried in sand but fresh.

Bhaijan notices the fish, picks it up, and returns to the center of the drama.

Even though the Priest has a lean and fragile body, he is still standing in the same position and the fear of the unknown staring from a skull's blank eyeholes, is enough to deter the whole crowd from countering him.

Bhaijan takes the knife lying with the kitchen utensils. Straight away he takes his pants off and starts cutting his thigh, there is already a deep cut mark on his thigh. He is murmuring some phrases in Arabic while cutting his flesh.

Blood is spilling all over the sand; some people cannot tolerate the gruesome cutting of flesh and vomit right there in the fire. No one notices that it is also a sin to spit on the charnel ground.

After an arduous struggle, Bhaijan cuts off a small piece of flesh. He puts it alongside the fish on dry leaves. It is tiny compared to the size of the fish.

"Let the scholar and purest amongst you come over and compare the weight of my flesh with that of the fish," the Priest orders without changing his posture.

"Stop it!" Shouts the person who was crying on Aghori's lap a while ago," this is enough! My mother, who died just yesterday, donated every useful piece of her body before dying, except the useless rotten skin and flesh and bones.

Now the last thing I want is that someone else pays the price for such an utterly nonsense rule of religion. Being the responsible son of the departed soul, I intend to give one of the most precious things in this world; one of the best teachings I learned from my mother." He says while sobbing and covering Bhaijan's wound with his own white rob.

"Even in the rarest of rare scenarios, if at all you have committed a mistake by cooking food to satisfy your hunger and by sheltering yourself in the warmth of my mother's burning bones, I forgive you. I don't judge you, and neither can I see you in pain at this great celebration of her life, when she will become one with Ganga Ma."

Everyone is shocked to hear the voice of this small boy. The Priest is so taken aback by the considerate and mindful reaction of the son that he abruptly returns to his normal persona.

The elderly man collects the kitchen utensils and other items the passengers have been using. The girl helps him gather all their belongings.

The boy continues to cry, as he picks out his mother's scattered bones from ashes, and puts them in a small bag. All the other people, including the Priest and Bhaijan are also busy collecting ashes from the ground.

The power of *forgiveness* is at work here. No reasonable person is able to raise any argument against this standalone word.

The mourners, after wiping the ground clean from ash, slowly proceed to the bank. The five basic elements of an identity are gone: the soul is unified with the sky; flesh has gone in the fire; water is one with the clouds; breath is returned back to the air. The bones and ashes are now heading to the earth beneath the ocean. The deceased's individuality is the only thing left in the memory of the near ones; even that will become ethereal in due course.

The Priest helps Bhaijan walk to the boat. Some people, who have been standing guarding the boat, move to give them some space to board. Bhaijan is struggling to step in and some people like us, just stand around like mute spectators of that struggle. We want to help, and there is something inside us that also pulls us to help, but there is something outside of us that pushes us back from that moment; the sense of being a common man or woman doesn't oblige us to help another common man or woman in need.

The elderly man invites the boy and other important people to board the boat so that they can immerse ashes in the middle of the river stream. The boy and other family members with sacks of ashes in their hands follow. Others, who did not take the opportunity to sit on the boat, do not like people from other religions interfering in the last rites.

"Do you ever ask the religion of a boatman on the Ghaat?" The Priest answers a question without waiting for it.

The passenger's boat slowly moves towards the center of the stream, and the Priest leads the prayer and guides the boy to immerse his mother's remains in the Ganga.

It is almost afternoon and they are moving with speed. The girl is holding the helm and the elderly man is helping Bhaijan dress-up his wound.

"Ohh Maa!" Bhaijan is in grueling pain," I never thought of bearing such pain in my life, after those painful days of my life."

"Don't worry Bhaijan. It will be alright, let me give you some opium, it will help you to imagine the pain has eased a bit," The elderly man says.

"If you don't want to use opium, you know that I have some grass." The Priest adds his sense of humor to the elderly's sense of care.

"Thanks for the offers, but I think I deserve this pain," Bhaijan politely refuses both offers. "I think it is the right time now that I share about my experience and goal of life."

He drags himself to the edge of the boat and leans against the wall.

"As such I am a nomad, most of the time I sleep on the boat and eat whatever I get from others. But, I am not a beggar."

"But, why did you offer your flesh when you are not even a Hindu?" The girl asks while steering the boat. She has become quite an expert in sailing now.

"That's part of my story. Actually, I am a Brahmin by birth but converted to Islam due to circumstances." Bhaijan continues. "I don't have a fancy 'on-the-edge' story behind me as you guys do.

I was a simple boy or maybe a girl from Baramulla in Kashmir: A northern most state of India, at the foothill of Mount Everest.

All of it began during the upsurge of militancy, or, the so-called freedom fighters struggle to set Kashmir free from India and Pakistan.

The story goes like this:

I was born to a Kashmiri Pundit but my father was also a popular Islamic scholar. Even mullahs from the Muslim community used to come to him for advice.

My mother died when she was giving birth to me, so for me, my father was my one and only hinge to this world.

My Adrushya Guru – if I can correlate it with my own voice – says that the mother is the most venerable for a kid. It is she, who shapes the body of a child to be ready to arrive in the world. She is the reason for existence in this world. At the same time, the father is the most important teacher in the world because he is the reason for our logical existence. He prepares us to face the world; he is the one who, along with the help of a mother, teaches us the rules of life.

In my case, apart from my arrival in this world, I owe everything else to my father: a devoted Kashmiri Brahmin with immense knowledge of Islam.

Many times, my father was coaxed to convert to Islam. However, as per him, there is hardly a difference between the two religions and even less was the necessity to change.

He used to fast in Ramadan; mourn the martyrdom of Imam Hussain (peace be upon him) by beating his chest during Muharram, and celebrate Diwali with full zest and zeal.

I was growing up in this ultra-liberated religious background, where Muslim kids could poke fun at Hindus and Hindus could do it to others in my presence. For kids, it was just a subject of bantering, not of any egoistic religious fanaticism. All parties in the game were there for naive laughter, and were sure that I was not going to spill the beans on any of them.

Evil does not belong to any particular religion, community or even country. It is just a disrupter. It does not like a well-regulated equilibrium that wise men set up for society to run smoothly. Evil is also very relative; something may be considered bad in one society but with valid justification it may be venerated as God-like in another. Interestingly, both are right in their individual contexts.

Both sides of the coin may be justified in one way or another. It becomes devilishly horrific when the two sides point fingers at each other. They should never meet each other because when they meet, it is a catastrophe for humanity.

My family, miss-happened to be the contorted mirror; where one aspect was able to look at the distorted reflection of the other.

✦ ✦ ✦ ✦ ✦ ✦

I still remember that fateful morning when I woke up in the hospital; I was in immense pain but still could hear the song that was playing in the hallway of our wooden house. Some eunuchs were dancing to the tune of drums in my fresh memory when it suddenly all became dark.

I was not able to move; I felt the sensation of pain coming from the bottom part of my belly though.

I saw my father sitting beside me and crying like a dark cloud. He still had the Tripund on his forehead and a skullcap was on his head. I was under the influence of sedatives so even though I could not be an active participant, I could witness everything happening in the room.

My situation was like an innocent witness in the court of justice, who knows he is right but cannot do anything to bring justice to the victims. I did not realize that it was *I*, who was the victim here. I did not know who the judge was and who the culprit was. My advocate, my father was helplessly yielding to our common fate.

It did not take much time for me to understand that now I would not be able to pee normally. I had to wear diapers even at the age of 12 years, and will have to continue wearing them for rest of my life perhaps.

The religious assemblies at home ceased soon thereafter. Our Persian carpet started to gather dirt. Its enlightened printed design, which used to shine due to the numerous fantastic conversations it had heard were fading in the darkness of ignorance.

Adrushya Guru says: people make a mistake when they do not remember God during their hay days, but then go crying to him when they see their life is out of control.

For my father, who used to follow the Almighty, even in the happiest and most prosperous days, he no longer had a place to go now. His social enigma was gone. In fact, he became the communal conflict for the two sides to clash against each other.

I, who used to follow him in quest of the ultimate truth, was left feeling even more confused. My recently inflicted physical challenges made my situation even worse.

It was winter. The snow in Baramulla was relatively more than in my previous eleven experiences. My father was cooking food to celebrate my twelfth birthday when the final nail of my predicament was hammered in. It was one of the cruelest turning points in my life. It left me nowhere but to figure out the only one thing – the goal of my life.

Some people need that final drastic push in their life, like the last straw which breaks the horse's back, in order to think about their life's goal

Someone knocked at our door. Innocent father, as usual, never bothered to check who the person was before opening the door. The miscreants lobbed grenades inside the house. One landed directly on my father's head. I can still see and hear the blast that blew up his skull. Is it expensive to be innocent?

Nobody claimed to know who did it, but I was mature enough to figure out the people behind it. There were Pundits who were not happy about what they considered as his over involvement in the Muslim community. On the other hand, Mullahs did not like him wearing a skullcap along with a Tripund. Some local leaders also found him to be the center of harmony, which they didn't like, because, for them, militants were the new tools for experimenting.

But, it didn't matter to me. On that day, I knew that if I, at all wanted to get away from the gangs of eunuchs and militants and priests and every other human being, then I had to run. I had to run no matter what; even if it meant that I would get stuck in the middle of nowhere and die a freezing and lonely death.

I picked my school bag and ran outside. I climbed a mountain. Then I realized that the fear of human monsters was slightly more compared to this brutal cold and snow. The beauty of snow disappeared for me. The prospect of being playful with it was lost forever. It was looking like an enemy to me now; like the people who had castrated me six years back.

Finally, I found shelter in a small cave that could provide at least some relief from the snow and bitter cold to me. I curled inside it and sat there the whole night in fear of more snow or a prowling snow leopard.

The morning was clear, and so was my focus to get out of there before anyone could find me. I slowly climbed down the cliff but my legs were automatically dragging me towards my town, as if they were missing their shoes. At every second turning point on my way to Srinagar, my feet kept making the opposite choice to my wanting to run away. They wanted me to go back to my town and find my father. I was a few yards away from my home when I heard people talking about my father and me. I had become an overnight Satan for my neighbors. People were talking about father as if he was the poorest father in the world, and me as the world's worst son.

I wanted to go straight home and tell all the people what had happened last night and what it meant to me. Why would I even think of killing my own father? He was the only precious thing in my life; the only reason for me to exist in this world.

Suddenly, someone covered me with a burqa from behind and pushed me into a small vehicle. The hands grabbing my face gave me the same weird sensation on my face that I had felt six years ago when I was castrated by the 'unknowns'. That incident changed my family's life forever. However, today, I was not afraid because there was no one left in my family. I was ready to jump in the ocean without worrying about anything or anyone. These people kept me nailed to the floor by literally sitting on top of me.

"You are on the path of liberation. Just let yourself flow with the time. Nothing will happen to you if you follow me," that is what the voice echoing in my ears was saying – It was that of my Adrushya Guru perhaps. He sounded like my father but I knew he was not.

"And what is my goal in the first place?" I enquired but did not receive any answer before my consciousness faded away.

I used to read in ancient scriptures that it is the most important responsibility of a son to ensure his father's mortal body is properly cremated, and his ashes are immersed in Ganga. That is the only way to repay the debt you owe to your parents. Son need to make sure that the person who is responsible for your being, the finger you held for the first time even before you understood the way of holding; the feet you followed before learning how to walk, the smile that gave you a sense of pride in doing something silly, the hair you pulled to balance yourself on your feet, are all recompensed for their service to you. You must see to it that with your own hands, you burn such a person into ashes or you turn him into soil by burying him in a grave with your own hands.

+ ◆ ◆ ◆ ◆ ◆ +

The next thing I remember is that I woke up in the red-light district of New Delhi. There, I was of high value, being a virgin minor eunuch. I was in demand for dancing to serving as a sex slave. I took that as my fate, and waited to receive the answer about my goal in life.

As time passed by, I discovered that there were many more kids like me who were forced into sex slavery in the market.

I remained there, confined, and as a slave until my value diminished to such a low rate that even a cup of tea was not affordable to me after selling me. It took five years for me to become so worthless that I could earn my partial freedom, which was invaluable to me. It is at times like this that valueless eunuchs like me gets their invaluable freedom to breathe in the open and walk on the streets.

My captors knew that they had trained my mind to enjoy the pain and harassment. They were confident that now I would become like a drug addict who must have some sorrow daily, some insult, and a pinch of bitterness to remain alive and happy. I am not blaming them however, because I think that is the goal of *their* life.

What these conspirators could not do, unbeknownst to them, is change my soul. Even at the most painful times of my life in Delhi's sex market, the question about my goal in life, remained kindled in my heart. My Adrushya Guru was still not willing to answer that. Maybe, I thought, he is dead and not bothered about me anymore to come back to me. But, I was wrong...

Even though I am a castrated eunuch, I still have the physical strength of a grown-up man. When I realized that, it emboldened me to become a tough person in the gang. After I lost all the value for my private parts, my next job was to become the one who is responsible for my current situation. I learnt that an eye for an eye is the rule and law of the land. If I am a eunuch of this quagmire, then I am supposed to take revenge by introducing as many boys and girls as possible, into the sex trade. In return, I would get the reward of complete freedom to roam across the country with no worry about money or food.

I took the offer happily. Not because of the vengeance in my mind, but because I was getting the opportunity to explore the world; maybe this was the start of my journey towards my goal.

The first assignment was to kidnap a girl from Southern India. My job was simply to mutilate the private parts of the girl kidnapped. For the rest of the activities, there were other gang members assigned.

After completing all the necessary preparations; our gang left for a small town close to southern India. It was the first time in my life that I was sitting on a train and it was such an awesome experience!! I used to dream about traveling on a train, but it was a distant dream due to the lack of facilities in my town, and an even farther daydream when I was in Delhi due to my self-created constraints. I still remember the night when I got back from the hospital and my father asked me what would make me happy, and I simply answered – a train ride.

I did not sleep for most of my journey and got down at every train-station to experience the small boy in me. The more I was travelling away from Delhi, the more I was becoming sensitive to myself – my Adrushya Guru.

Finally, I got off, close to my destination of Villuparam. I further travelled to a small town called Koovagam, alone only with myself. To my utter surprise, this village was beyond my imagination, it was nothing like the towns on hills. I could see a confluence of eunuchs from all over the world in this small town. Right from the station platform to the city center, I could see only eunuchs and transgender people around me.

It has been a while since I switched to Islam now, and actually, thanks to my upbringing, it does not matter too much to me by then. I was more liberated than constrained, I could offer Namaaz to Krishna or even chant praises to him in Arabic.

My task in the whole operation was to castrate a young girl and return to base.

Who is the girl? Who is going to bring her? Who is going to take care of her afterwards? What if she escapes after castration, what if she dies from bleeding? I was not supposed to worry about any such issues. In fact, I had only two minutes to go inside, perform the castration and leave, no questions; no turning back; every member in the gang would be performing their own task.

It was my first assignment but I had already seen so much blood and violence by then, that I thought it would be just another task for me.

The crowd and frenzy in the town was mesmerizing and distracting from my task. I asked one of the eunuchs in town what the occasion was, and he looked at me with sweet disgust. Sweet, because he was not offended by my ignorance of one of the most coveted festivals for people who are transgender, and at the same time, disgusted that even after being a eunuch, I was not aware of such an important occasion.

He explained to me about the festival. It was the mass marriage of eunuchs. I had never heard of it in my whole life, before, or even after becoming a eunuch.

"Today is the day when we get married to King Aravan!" He literally shouted but I could not hear properly due to the high pitch noise in the air.

I asked him again and this time he grabbed me by my hand and took me to the center of the procession. There was a nice statue of a king and well-dressed eunuch brides were busy tying conjugal knots with the king. I even saw Muslim eunuchs queued to be married, without any hatred or discrimination against each other.

"Who was this king?" I asked my prompt guide.

"What do you mean by – was? He is here, and he will be here, forever," he retorted sarcastically with a smile. "King Aravan is the only one in this whole universe who had this great honor to be the husband of the Lord of the Lords, Vishnu!"

"Ohh! Now I get it! He is the one-night husband of Mohini – one of the twenty-four incarnations of the Lord Vishnu!" I responded positively with the sense of self-pride for the knowledge.

"I don't know about Mohini Avatar of Vishnu but what I do know is that he happened to be the one and only man in this world who got married to Lord Vishnu as his wife. So, we come here and marry King Aravan at least once in our life. This puts not us but Lord Vishnu at par with us," he showed his innocence.

"Let me tell you the story quickly," I opened up the conversation while looking at my watch. I knew I still had some time before my part was to be played in the heinous act I agreed to be part of.

"When Mahabharata, the epic war between truth and falsehood was about to begin, the Pandavas got divine instruction to sacrifice one of their dear ones to ensure success in the war. This sacrifice was not to show that they are superstitious, but to ensure that they go to war with an open mind; that they go and fight while ensuring the sacrifice made by them does not go in vain, and they fight with full commitment. And above all, to make sure that there is nothing more important than to defend the ultimate truth in this world.

There was no one, including warrior Pandavas, brave enough to come forward and put his life on the sword for this noble cause. Finally, King Aravan presented himself with just one condition, and that was to marry the most beautiful girl in this world for just one day.

Krishna, the incarnation of Vishnu at the time, was overwhelmed by the sense of self-sacrifice by King. He took the form of Mohini, the most beautiful woman in the universe – His other incarnation which he had taken only twice earlier. Mohini married King Aravan for one night. The king kept his promise and sacrificed himself next day morning. Before the martyrdom, Krishna blessed him with this amazing gift to marry the most beautiful living beings in this world every year. Krishna also blessed him with the honor that even though Pandavas would conquer the war, it would still be King Aravan, the only one from the descendants of the great King Bharat, who will be worshipped until the end of time.

Now look at us, one of the most beautiful beings of this world, who marry King Aravan every year. We are also the ones at par with Lord Vishnu. There is no one else who shares a husband with him," I concluded my knowledge of this ancient history.

"You are right, King Aravan did nothing but follow the goal of his life he put himself under a sword just to make sure that he achieves what he wants, and look at the result: he is the beloved one for all of us for centuries, and he will continue to be until the end of time."

✦ ✦✦✦✦ ✦

For the very first time in my life, I felt proud to be a eunuch. I wanted to be a part of the ritual now. I thought that if this can give me a sense of being for someone, then I will be more than happy to live like a bride in this world, even if it is just for one day.

A very familiar and scary hand pulled me back from joining the makeshift dressing room to become a bride. The angry eyes reminded me of my incomplete task. I am sure the person who pulled me out was not a eunuch because there was no way that any person of my cast could get away from such an enigmatic occasion.

His stare jolted my confidence upside down. My soul was shaking because I could still see his hand on my shoulder and the feeling was same as the one I had when I lost my boyhood; when I was deprived of being a child irrespective of the notion of gender. This same touch ended my father's spirit, and any wish to live in this world like a human being.

I was shivering with fear as well as from the weakest form of anger. I wanted to rip this hand apart from the body and eat it. However, I could not even move an inch from where I was standing.

"You have two minutes. Go in the building right across the street. The girl is already in the only ladies' toilet on the second floor," he whispered in my ear and melted away in the crowd.

We have such great consciousness about what we want to hear. I was not able to listen to a shouting fellow just a few moments before, but right now, I could clearly hear every word of a whisper from the impending danger.

A slave man inside me dragged myself towards the building. On the other hand, a liberated woman pulled me towards my would-be and eternal husband.

I was standing in the middle of a crowd physically, but I was nowhere emotionally. People were rustling all around me. The man inside me became stronger and finally pulled me towards my eluding freedom. It did not like me to be bound to a statue; it did not want me to be dependent and live in a confined identity of a wife. I gave in to him and stormed into the toilet.

It was a small and dirty toilet. An unconscious naked girl was lying on the floor. Her body was smeared with urine and in the colors of the ongoing celebration. She didn't appear to belong to this part of the world. I was callous to her pain until I took out a tool to finish my job and attain my freedom. Somewhere deep in my heart, the child in me forced me to realize what pain this girl was going to go through, how many times her father would have to die before he would give up; how many times this innocent girl would be brutalized for making just one mistake - a mistake committed as an attempt to know this world. A mistake committed to have a sense of liberty by leaving her mother's finger in a crowded market.

I am sure even animals do this and even more sure that they feel pride in leaving their baby's hand, to make the child independent. However, it is so different with another species of animals called humans.

Even though she was a girl, I could still assimilate myself with her. I could see that I would have been the same age as her when I was castrated. I did not know the pain of castration, just as she is also not going to experience it, but, I still remember the first encounter with the vultures who wanted to show their menial power on a helpless and hapless innocent kid. I still start sweating when I think about the gruesome second experience of having a fully-grown man inside a small fissure in my body. Yes, that's right, the second experience, because for the first time I did not even know what to expect. It was the second time, when I knew what was going to happen and how painful it was going to be. Above all, the fear of that pain was the actual experience for me.

Tears rolled out of my eyes and the tool dropped to the floor. Someone knocked on the door, "Is it done?" I remember this voice. I had no option now. However, the child in me was still afraid of this voice.

"One minute!" I replied with shaking hands.

"Do it quick!!" He shouted at me.

I picked up the tool and cut my thigh as deep as I could. The sharp tool was smeared with blood. Then I penetrated the girl's private part, first with my finger to make sure she is not hurt, and then I carefully inserted the tool so that it looks like it is inside, but not hurting her. I smeared my blood around her private parts just to make it look like it is blood from her body.

The door opened with a bang and I could see the angry person entering the toilet.

He was very irritated. He banged my head against the wall. He must have prayed to his angels that I did not have the tool in my hand; otherwise he would have been hanging on his last breath that day.

He inspected the girl and even before I could react, he further inserted the tool and turned it around brutally, just to make sure that the job was done properly. I shouted due to the agonizing pain in my soul. I felt like all my efforts to save one kid from losing her identity had gone in vain. The man's face and hand were covered with blood but his face remained without any expressions. He did not have any sorrow, or fear, or anger, or even happiness in his eyes; they were simply blank and staring at infinite. He tried to clean his face with his already bloody hands only to make his face even bloodier.

I was standing in the corner, looking at him with horror, when the girl almost awoke out of the sedation and started to moan a little in pain.

"Huh!" He shouted and kicked the small and fragile body of the girl.

"Now don't just stand here as per your character; leave this shit place as soon as possible."

He rushed out of the toilet as I stood there, petrified. I was bleeding, so was the girl and her cries were getting louder and louder. Perhaps, her grinding screams were only penetrating my ears, as no one else came to the toilet to take a look inside.

Finally, I got the courage to pick up the girl and hold her in my lap. She was crying relentlessly now. Due to the loss of blood she became unconscious shortly, but her intermittent sobs were enough to shake me from inside. The already loud sound of bands and music was growing every second now.

It is such an old incident but I can live and relive every moment of that day even today.

I took the tool out of her body and put it in my pocket. The clotted wound was dry now.

I was still crying and did not want to leave her, but I was then forced by the Kaali inside me to find and kill that animal.

The marriage ceremony was in the last stage and there was just one special set of the dresses left. Everyone was looking for the eligible volunteer eunuch to come and wear the final dress. It was all black dress and makeup. Being a eunuch, I knew how to prepare quickly for thirty minutes of suicide of the soul. I moved to the center and picked up the dress. All of a sudden, the whole procession went silent; everyone was looking at me- some were shocked, others were happy, and a very few had tears in their eyes.

I did not know what had just happened. A few eunuchs came forward to help me get ready. I stripped my clothes and few of the assistant eunuchs fainted after looking at my bloody thigh and the big hole at my private part.

I dressed myself in a black sari and blouse with all black makeup. My grown-up hair was flirting with the sweat and wind now. Kaali had entered my soul, and the anger was evident in my eyes. The silence was louder than the bands playing.

As soon as I came out of the covers, the music exploded at a thunderous volume. The eunuch, who had brought me to the procession earlier in the day, approached me and gave a very tight and warm hug.

I asked her to help me find the man who had pulled me out of the procession earlier. She came back, with three other eunuchs' holding the man, within no time. Although he was beaten badly, he was still laughing at me.

"Do you know what you have just done?" He laughed sarcastically at my ignorance.

"Do you know what I am just about to do?" I laughed at his laughter and ignorance about his impending but unaware death.

"Being the chosen black widow eunuch, you need to finish the ceremony before you can do anything else, you will get one final wish at the end," the head of the procession interrupted me from further arguing with him.

"But," I blacked out before I could speak, and there I was, standing in front of myself in the black sari with dark blood trickling out of my forehead.

It was my Adrushya Guru telling me: "Now you have your goal, the girl is more precious than your life. Go and follow your path. You are destined to achieve your goal and subsequently myself." I told myself.

"But, what?" The head shouted back at me.

"Don't let this donkey get away, he is my last wish."

"But Mausi!" Another Eunuch tried to intervene but it was too late. We were moving towards the Idol of King Aravan.

I was slowly transforming into a different world; an enchanted one. Dancing and lunging towards the statue of King Aravan. I could see my actions but I did not have control over myself.

My body and mind were floating in the unknown. I was walking beside me and crying out loud. Still, I was happiest person in the town. The slowly rising noise of cries, sobs and mourning made me crazy.

I reached the small truck which was holding the idol of King Aravan; he himself had stopped playing his flute to help me board his chariot. I hugged him tight. I still feel his warmth. All the voices around me had faded by now. Everyone was envious of me when I stood up there with King Aravan. Everyone was crying and so jealous of me. The less fortunate eunuchs carefully started throwing shoes and sandals at me. They didn't want to hurt Aravan. Nonetheless, *I* was enjoying the company of King Aravan. He was pure and as clean as Ganga. His blue body decorated with jewels was indescribable. His big, hypnotic eyes were enough to pull anyone out of any misery of this world. There was no pain in the world that could break my spell with ultimate reality and bring me to the falsehood of this world. I was in singularity and nothing else mattered to me.

The procession was moving slowly and so were my feelings, until I realized that I had suddenly raised my hand with the tool in my hands and hit Aravan hard on his head. He was bleeding, his crown had fallen down but his smile was still intact. His eyes were still admiring me without complaining. They were oozing with unconditional love.

I looked around in despair. I could see the people who were envious of me just a moment ago, were now shouting in anger at me. I was behaving like a demon and the happiness expressed on my face was inflicting further pain upon them.

I was not concerned after hurting the one who has made us and who can kill us in the blink of an eye. The persona, who had given true happiness just a minute ago, is mortally dead. Nevertheless, I was excited to see that others were going to die without having this ultimate experience and it is going to put me apart from the league of these cockroaches. I turned around and hit the idol until it was completely broken.

People were throwing themselves under the wheels of the truck and committing suicide. Some of them were throwing stones and knives at me. This time, I did not have King Aravan around to save me. It was me, who had to save myself now.

The head eunuch priest stopped the chariot and pulled me down by my hair. I fell down on the road.

People turned upon me and started thrashing me. Some of them tore up my sari and blouse. I was laughing in pain and bearing the full brunt of the unpardonable crime I had just committed. I could still see the smiling head of King Aravan lying on the street. For others, it was simply a piece of the clay, but I could still see him with those smiling lips.

Truly, it is our perception that builds and destroys God in this world. He cannot exist without us. We make Him and then expect Him to do miracles; we the creators become beggars in front of our own imagination; is this reality of our life? Does this happen with the ultimate creator of this world as well?

I was completely naked and scarred, when the head eunuch stopped people from thrashing me to the death. The music abruptly stopped; crying turned into sobbing, and tarmac of the road and the sweltering sunrays were mixing with my blood to smell like hell.

The head priest moved towards me with a small tool in his hands, and a clear intention to finish me right there. I spread my legs, knowing the type of death I am going to get. I also knew it is less painful if it happens quickly and for that, one's legs must spread as far as possible. He raised his hand to hit me with the special tool but stopped just before penetrating it into my private parts.

He saw the fresh wound on my thigh and became angry at his bodyguards. Apparently, they cannot kill a body with a wound but they can easily hurt a soul and inflict thousands of wounds upon it.

The group of old eunuchs asked me about my last wish. But even before I could tell them, I saw the crushed head of my target under the chariot wheels. I asked them to handover the girl to me. It was unprecedented in their tradition to have someone injured performing the last rites and even more so, a person asking for a girl as the gift just before his death.

The group had a detailed discussion with the chief before picking me up and dumping me in the truck. It was done so surreptitiously that no one in the crowd could figure out what happened in the middle.

One of the elder eunuchs changed his appearance to look like me; he smeared himself with my blood and lay down on the road. Other members of the inner coterie hit him with stones and knives until he became unrecognizable. Then the head eunuch killed him with the tool. This was the sacrifice done to keep the tradition intact.

I was watching the situation unfolding from the small fissure in the truck's lid. I could clearly see that the elderly eunuch left hardly any space for easy penetration and it must have been very painful for him.

I was not able to distinguish whether it was happening in reality or in my dreams.

***

The next morning, when I woke up, I found myself on a train with the girl sleeping on the opposite seat. I could feel some known strangers sitting around me.

I was on my way to Banaras now!

Months passed by before I recovered from the mental and physical hardship of that day, but now when I look back, I think it summarizes the whole of my life in those couple of hours. I used to live as a caretaker in a widow shelter in Banaras, and the girl, who hardly knew about marriage apart from as a game played with a toy king and queen was registered there as a child widow from Kolkata.

I raised her as my own child while hiding the fact that I was a eunuch, until one fine day, when a woman came out of nowhere and claimed the girl as her child. She took the girl away from me and I could not do anything about it.

I was completely broken down after losing her, until I met Aghori, and finally you.

My Adrushya Guru had not spoken to me until our meeting at

the Pundit's home. He literally woke me up that night and told me to be ready to travel on a long journey. I am not sure whether it is just a fascination of mine to meet my girl there, or something else but the mere thought of going on this journey stokes butterflies in my belly."

As Bhaijan winds up his story and returns to his present, the boat on the river is shaking hard due to a strong wind.

Everyone: the girl, the Priest, and the elderly man in the group were all lost in the time and space of Bhaijan's memoir. Some have tears while others are looking with blank eyes at the dusky sky to find the director of this drama called life.

Yet another day is over for them. Their boat is crossing the border with Bengal and the smell of the maverick artists of Bengal is filling the air above river. Faint clouds of moist are once again coming back home with a blanket of darkness which is ready to put Ganga to sleep for the night.

Bhaijan sleeps in Joan's lap. The Priest is in a meditative state, while the elderly man steers the boat towards an unknown destination. The silence prevailing on the boat hides the commotion brewing inside the three souls. It was decided that tonight is the night of journeying and the boat is not going to stop. Everyone's spirit is so full of emotions, that no one felt the need to satisfy their hunger.

Typical Robindra Sangeet is emanating from distant villages to fill the void left by the sleeping moist in the air.

They have just crossed Midnapore and are heading towards Hubli now, the last town before entering the City of Joy – Kolkata.

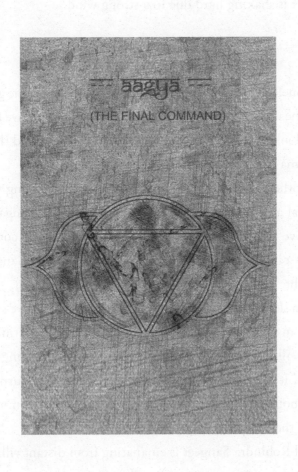

aagya

(THE FINAL COMMAND)

--- AAGYA ---
(THE FINAL COMMAND)

It is early in the morning and the river stream is just waking up to fiddle with the sunrays like a violin in an orchestra. The width of the river has grown exponentially, converting into a giant lake in this part of India.

"Slow down, and dock here!" The commanding order breaks the spell of the common dream of all the passengers.

Someone with an obese voice is shouting from outside and forcibly guiding the boat to embark at the small dock.

Assuming it is the usual morning tea break for the elderly man, Bhaijan comes out to join him, only to learn that it is actually the police commandeering them to stop at a waterway police station for enquiries.

"Kee Holo Hawildar Babu Moshay (what happened)?!" Bhaijan enquires from the boat while sending a signal inside the cabin that danger lies ahead.

The Priest suddenly jumps to his feet and picks up his skull, full of ash from the Charnel Island. He rubs the ash all over the body of sleeping girl, and also quickly applies a red mark on her forehead.

Colors are such a fascinating treasure in this world; they can hide anything in their disguises. Anyone can be a chameleon and change his colors to suit the environment and to save one from potential dangers.

It took no time at all for an African American woman to convert to being a seasoned Aghori, just by applying a small amount of human ashes on her body and make her hair look like a sadhu's.

"Who is inside?" The Police Officer who has just boarded their boat shouts at the elderly man.

"You can check yourself," Bhaijan answers while leaving the interpretation inside the cabin doors.

The officer slowly opens the door by using his stick – a typical weapon of defense used by Indian police.

Yes, it is true that color can help in hiding your appearance but when a soul starts speaking to another soul in its naked world, nothing can hide behind clothes or hues; especially, when the conversation is happening between a culprit and a commander.

"That lady is fraud! She is not an Aghori!" The Police Officer shouts and raises his stick to hit the girl.

"Can I speak to Binoy Babu?" The elderly man speaks calmly from outside.

The shouting constable stops before hitting the girl and turns back towards the deck.

"Ki Holo!" He shouts at the elderly man.

"Can I speak to Binoy Babu?" The elderly man repeats his request.

Again, a conversation of a soul with another does not leave any space for assumptions and probabilities. Their words and the weight in those words are always binary, you have the answer or you do not have one, it's a simple: yes or no.

The constable reads the elderly man's eyes and learns that it is not a regular boat.

"What are you guys up to?" The constable diverts the enquiry with an attempt to let them go.

"Ask Ganga or ask the water." The elderly man is at peace.

He sees some people are rushing towards the boat with cans of fuel and some other packets.

"Water goes to Bangladesh and Ganga goes to Kolkata, where do you want to go?" The constable recognizes the faces approaching the boat and he becomes like a tamed sheep now.

"Water goes to the ocean and it doesn't matter if it goes via Kolkata or via Bengal. Ganga remains here, in our hearts," the elderly man replies.

The group of people have reached the boat. They quickly get busy in filling the boat with fuel and cleaning it up.

There is also a fresh supply of food brought by them.

"Where is Binoy Babu?" The elderly man brings the discussion back to his original request.

"Don't worry about Sahib. Just give me the message and I will convey it to him," the constable replies in a hurry. "Just let me know and I can take you through the gate." He winds up his discussion before waiting for an answer, "The current is too strong in the main river so I will not recommend taking the main stream if you want to go to Bengal but it's your choice," he advises.

"Then show us the path," the elderly asks him.

"Sure, if you still insist on going to Bengal then give me 10 minutes, I can get all the gates closed to bring the current under control," he further advises.

"But that will kill a lot of people upstream who have just started recovering from the flood," the elderly man argues with him in his calm voice.

"Who cares about them?"

"Well, you should," the elderly man responds calmly.

"Seriously? If that is the case, then why are you threatening me to comply with your choice?" The constable feels a bit stronger from the inside now.

"I was not threatening you. It is your assumptive brain that pushed you to the habitual part of your attitude – to be afraid, to yield." The elderly man smiles at him "I know Binoy Babu very well. I wanted to cut short my conversation with you because I understand that I can get what I want by simply talking to him, instead of explaining to you about who my passengers are, their religion, their nationality and so on," He concludes. "Anyway I want to go to Kolkata, and certainly don't want to kill people upstream."

"OK, I will get you through the canal gate now," the constable who is a bit in himself, suggests.

The elderly man signals to his men to leave; they follow his orders promptly.

The boat starts moving on its journey again. It does have a destination, but that is not important, the experience of the journey is a must for an individual to attain his or her destiny.

They enter into a bypass artery of the barrage. The Police constable standing at the front is enough for the boat to sail through without any checks and marks. The elderly man serves fresh breakfast to all in the boat. The eager and hungry faces are clearly showcasing that last night went by without dinner.

Passengers in the boat are silent as usual with the only music playing being the occasional chirps from birds in trees.

"Now you are in Hubli, Ganga has gone to Bengal," the constable says jokingly while signaling one of the passing by security boats to come towards theirs.

"In another hundred kilometers, you will find Kushti Lake, just turn to your left from there and follow the stream," the constable advises. "Also, you should not speak in Bengali from here onwards, or else you will be caught easily," he points to Bhaijan.

"One final thing, there is no Binoy Babu in Farakka now. He was killed in a gang war last month," this time the constable is looking at the elderly man. "And even though the water is going to the ocean, the right direction for you is to go to Bengal. Don't go to Kolkata. The girl and Aghori both are in danger. Some savages are looking to hunt them at the first opportunity that becomes available."

He signals the boatman to cruise away without waiting for their answers. The elderly man smiles at him. Once again, he seeks the narrator of this story – called life in the deep blue sky.

The Priest and girl are still sitting with their Aghori makeup on.

"Going forward, nobody speaks unless I allow it. We are entering in a foreign land. This is Bengal and you will not find the best in the people here. They are like tigers of Sundarban, very beautiful from the outside but protective from their nature." The elderly man puts forward some strict guidelines for the team.

They spend the rest of the day keeping a watch on the lake to turn towards Bengal. Finally, just before dusk, they find the obscure diversion and carefully tread away in the shallow stream of the water of Hugli River.

Their boat is slowly moving towards the uncertain unknown. The one thing that is certain though, is that they are moving downstream. Bhaijan switches off the boat and lets it follow the stream. The bushes and trees are making eerie sounds. It's a completely desolated land; very strange for the riverbank, to be full of trees but no birds. It is clear from the half-gazed grass, that all the creatures living around there have left the place in a hurry.

"Let's dock the boat somewhere here. It's good plain ground. We also have ample water in the stream, just in case of any emergency, to sail off quickly," the elderly man suggests and all agree to it, except the Priest, who suggests they continue until they reach the column of smoke visible ahead.

Others acknowledge that the Priest needs a charnel ground for his prayers.

It takes another thirty minutes for them to reach a small nook in the river where a freshly lit up funeral pyre is burning.

The sun has already set far in the west now and the toll on their body and spirit is clearly visible. The heat from the burning wood is now carrying invigorating feelings when mixed with the breeze coming from the river.

Everyone is busy in their usual silent conversation and completing their regular tasks to prepare for dinner. Yet again, their oven is going to be a funeral fire.

The Priest completes his task of moving all the stuff for cooking. He then goes to the other side to take a dip in the water. His skull pot is with him and Breach is following him like a scared kid follows his mother. He leaves one of his wooden-bead chains on an unnoticed trident installed a few yards away from the fire.

The whole area is piercingly silent. Even the creepy water is afraid to make any sound and it seems as if it is in a haste to pass by this area. The only audacious noises in the atmosphere are coming from the fire. It is a mixed noise of the cracking wood and the slowly turning red-hot bones. It appears that the sticks are at their last stage so they do not have any fear of death; the skeleton of the human being has just witnessed the inevitable so it has already experienced the beauty of it.

Occasionally, some utensils are colliding with each other to screech through the sheet of silence. Bhaijan, who is not able to walk well, is sitting quietly while preparing a piece of meat for dinner. The girl, whose night starts early, just after late afternoon, is looking at the infinite skyline above the water stream, and the elderly man is again on his own to find someone in the blackish blue horizon.

The darkness is wrapping everything around the fire very fast. The flames are dancing above the bones in the celebration of life and in the excitement of embarking on another journey.

It is true that reaching our destination, and achieving the goal set before us matters somewhat to prove ourselves to others. However, the journey to the destination matters the most of all to our own self. Above all that is what matters most. One can succeed or not in achieving a tangible result of the journey, but the journey itself has just one outcome, and that is experience.

The ballet of flames is showing that this outcome of one's journey is the only thing that a soul carries forward to the next voyage. The goal achieved earlier, the destination attained in our current life ends just here. Its boundary is limited to only one phase of life whereas experience goes beyond.

"Bam-Bam!!" A loud shout by the Priest stirs up silence, as well as the tired bodies around the pit-fire. The shakeup also brings emancipated residents of those bodies back in to their dual reality.

The girl is able to see through the flames that the Priest is standing on one foot. His one hand is resting on the trident and holding skull in the other. His long, black hair is unraveled and fluttering in wind. He is covered in the hot ash from the funeral pyre. Some of the small fire flakes are still sparkling like red light on his deeply tanned skin. A strange aura has engulfed the sky around his body. His eyes are fiery red. The fully-grown beard is failing to hide the glow of his face.

His mere presence is enough for the blazes to jump even higher without any encouragement from the insignificant wind.

He is staring at the passengers curled together. They in turn are looking at him with fearful veneration. Breach is standing right beside him with a small but living golden snake in her mouth.

"Just so you know; I have to have a conversation with the embarking one!" He literally screams at them. "You are most welcome to experience it, but at your own risk!"

"What is the risk?" The girl reverts.

"SSHHH!" Bhaijan forces her to keep quiet.

"No! No one is no one's guide here. Everyone has his or her own path as well as destiny. It is just a matter of predefined coincidence that we are traversing on the same route for some moments; this does not give anyone the right to impose his or her own rules on the others; at the same time, it is our duty to respect each other's choice. For Allah is the same for all of us and It has already given the right powers to us to move towards It," the elderly man intervenes.

"Satya Vachan! (You are right!)," the Priest conforms to his views. "The next few hours are going to unfold like you have never seen before. It is going to be a bit frightening for the ignorant whereas interesting for the worthies. I am warning you again: if you think worldly logic is the only way to go, then, you belong to the boat. No one will bother you, not even the sound or wind only if you chose to go back to the boat. But, if you think you are open to receive each and everything the way it comes, rather than asking how it comes, then hold your breath," the

148

Priest explains in a relatively quieter voice. "But, here I warn you again: Do Not Say a Word, not even a single sound should come out of your body until I say so or we will be departing to the other world by sunrise."

No one moves from their respective positions, but simply nod their heads in agreement; the silence zone is in effect immediately.

It is such a wonderful chance to experience, when we put logic aside and take every moment as it occurs to us. Rationality simply defines why something has happened, and analysis describes how it has happened. Time helps to show when it happened. However, what has happened is nothing, other than our experience. It is the fourth dimension. Everyone in this world asks; what is at the left and right-hand side of a zero to assess his or her profit and loss, but no one tries to enquire what is inside it.

Once we start thinking, about 'what' without its implications, we liberate ourselves from the duality of this world. Nothing, be it religion, faith, truth, falsehood, or even our own existence, matters to us in this quest of – What.

The Priest waits for a few moments before closing his eyes. He is still standing on one leg. His posture is like that of a pillar of faith standing for thousands of years, holding the sky up for us. The cracking sound of the burning wood logs and bones is again dominating the air.

The passengers feel like someone is walking behind them. They do not have the courage to turn around however. The girl is scared, she knows the unknown ghost behind them is far more dangerous than the known devil standing in front of her; her blindness has taught her this lesson very well.

The snake entangled in Breach's canines is slowly slithering down to the sand. The wind is gradually picking up its pace. First, the passengers hear the whisper of the wind. Perhaps it is telling them to run away to the boat before what is about to start, begins; then, they feel the breeze wiping their face to wake them up from the slumber of the so-called – reality of this world. A sudden and strong gust pulls them out from their feet and throws them on the sand. All three of them hold each other's hands to be heavy enough to not blow away in the impending storm.

A sudden silence and vacuum ensues, making it seem as if they were tested for their physical defiance and they have succeeded to earn the next chapter unfolding.

———————————— ✦ ✦ ✦ ✦ ✦ ✦ ————————————

Out there on the other side of the pyre, the snake is slowly crawling towards them. It marks a clear circle around them in the sand and then returns back to the Priest. It starts slithering up and on the Priest. His eyes are still half-closed. The snake slowly wraps itself around the neck of the Aghori, who looks like Shiva standing in the middle of his abode: the Shmasaan.

The girl looks to the other side to check her vision. She realizes that this is the third time in the last couple of weeks that she is able to see clearly in the dark. She sees her Kaali Avatar sitting right next to her and smiling. "Be strong to experience what is about to happen now with open heart and mind. Don't get distracted by the fear of uniting with me; be courageous to feel what you deserve," Kaali advises her. She nods in agreement and turns her head to look back at the drama of lively death unfolding.

The snake is slowly trying to enter in the left nostril of the Priest. A small tickle of fear forces the girl to close her fist in the sand, Kaali, sitting beside her, stops her from doing so. The nod of her head in disagreement calms the girl down.

The snake is about three feet long and at least four inches thick but still keeps going inside the Aghori's nose effortlessly.

There is almost a foot of tail left when the snake starts wagging it and tightens it around Aghori's neck. There is a bloody red tinge on the other nostril of the Aghori.

Bhaijan tries to stand up but is forced by the elderly man to stay where he is.

A little bit of movement of the red hue on the Priest's lip clears the suspicion; it is not blood but a two-pronged tongue flickering from the inside. Finally, the snake's head comes out of the other nostril for a moment. It is staring with anger at Bhaijan, as if it has sensed his movement.

The stoning gaze, continues for almost five minutes. The movement of its tail and forked tongue is clearly portraying the aggression in its nature. Bhaijan is frozen like ice, even the sweat on his forehead is refusing to follow the law of gravity. The snake slowly retracts in the nostril. For the very first time Aghori opens his mouth and here comes the snake out of it, the remaining tail slides inside while the front body emerges out of Aghori's mouth.

Everyone is so focused on the snake and its movements, they don't realize that the burning skeleton is slowly turning in the fire; his hands and legs are stretching like a person waking up after a long and peaceful sleep.

Breach immediately becomes like a soldier, ready to attack to defend the Priest. The snake coils itself inside Aghori's mouth, placing itself deep in his throat. It then slings itself out of Aghori's mouth, flying and making a blaring screech like a hawk. It lands in the fire and ties itself around the moving feet of the skeleton.

The eyes of the spectators following the snake's projectile catch the next shock of their life – The incinerated skeleton they thought was a dead body, is moving!

For a moment, the passengers think this is a suicide attempt by the snake and the conversation of the Priest is over in some overt way by having the snake inside himself. Perhaps the Priest wanted to show off his talent. However, they were not ready to gauge what was lying ahead of them. The skeleton jumps up and stands up its feet. It tries to lunge towards the Priest when Breach prepares herself to counter any attack, but the skeleton body falls down flat as its feet have been tied by the snake.

"You may stand up, but don't move an inch!" The expression-less Priest orders the skeleton.

It slowly stumbles and tries to keep its balance with a little gap in its foot bones. A six-foot-tall body of fire is standing between the passengers and the Priest. Breach is standing guard; the snake has turned into ashes but it is still tied like a shackle made of steel.

"Why are you not leaving for your next destination?" The Priest questions the skeleton.

"I need some answers from you before moving to the next step."

"And what if I were not going by this way?"

"Huh, you know, I am at a position where the past, present and future; time and space are mere toys lying in front of me. They are in a form that cannot be defined for mortal beings," it sits down on the fire-bed as if it is a comfortable couch and starts untying the shackles of snake bones around its feet.

"I know that the goal of your life was to come and answer my questions, which I have been asking for centuries. I also know the people sitting behind me are just instruments instigating you to come here. I also know that the next few hours are going to be guiding factors for these passengers.

What do you think? Why did the police constable let you go? Why was the honest officer, Binoy Babu, killed in a gang war? Who changed the mind of the brothel head to allow you to take the girl with you, even though she was a milking cow for the business? Who spared Bhaijan from imminent death in the eunuch's only marriage function? Why did the old man only get to go to Patna as the place to hide, in this whole world?

What was the reason that your brainchild failed in its first attempt and you never got another chance to prove yourself in the fraternity of intellectuals – who talk about the limitless world but still confine themselves with the presumptions of always being inside some boundaries?

Above all, you may not know, even I cannot tell you what actually your goal in life is. It is hiding behind the apparent one you are chasing right now with these known strangers. Some things only become clear after they are experienced, and experience comes only after we live through such things."

The skeleton kneels down and takes out a stone like red-hot object with a bluish tinge from the remains of the snake's ashes.

"So, what is the question?" The Priest asks

"Will you answer or not?" The body tries to assure itself, "This is my eleventh attempt in the quest of finding the answer. Every attempt was a step closer in my quest. Sometimes I was not ready with enough experience and the other times you were not available to answer. I was enjoying myself until now, because I was getting the opportunity to visit this unique and worldly experience – Life"

"So, what is the question?" The Priest continues to ask the same question, "I am not sure I will be able to answer, but I can assure you that I will try my best. If my duty is to serve you, or if your goal depends on me and this is the right time, then I am sure the answer will come out of my universe automatically. But," the Priest blinks his eye for the first time and that blink proves to be deadly as it gives enough time to the skeleton to run havoc on the ground.

The whole place, except inside the circle where the passengers are quivering in fear of the unknown, becomes filled with venomous snakes and lizards in a jiffy. Snakes are raining from the trees; scorpions are crawling all over Breach and the Priest. Some of the snakes are hissing with poisonous teeth glaring in the light of the flames. A few are ready to lunge on the passengers and devour them. Their jaws, spawned open from north-south are large enough to swallow all three of them in one gulp. The passengers feel like they are in a prehistoric reptile zoo – the only difference being that they are the ones inside an invisible glass cage.

"Ha-ha, but what?" The skeleton asks sarcastically.

The Priest opens his eyes and the snakes start retreating from his and Breach's bodies. The entire ground is still infested with different types of snakes, and reptiles.

"But, what I see is that even though you say you are ready, you are still not keen to hear the answer," the Priest objects to the attack on him. "And, I am not interested in answering just for your entertainment. No one here is looking for fun. Our caravan is earning what you call life. You have left it behind; the quest here and now is for them to achieve their goal."

"Perhaps you are right, I am afraid of the ultimate unknown. I know that this is the right time and I am going to get answer no matter what. Nevertheless, I have been delaying it for the last ten days. Ever since I have been placed on the fire bed, I am not allowing it to evaporate me in the thin ether. I am stuck in the – 'to-be in the flickering past' or 'to-be in the eternal present' perhaps.

I am in the final dilemma of duality. However, I also know that it is inevitable for me to move on. So please, answer my question and let's see if I catapult into the infinite or bounce back with yet another milestone I am required to achieve for my soul before the journey ends."

The Priest, who is still standing on one foot, and has his eyes half open reacts to the slight movement by the elderly man inside the circle: his toe is about to come out of the circle and a giant cobra is ready and waiting to grab the opportunity to do what it is best at.

The seeming danger for the mortals in the circle; the finite thought of their existence in the world; and the fear of death is causing them to keep breathing in their small world within the circle and keep on modifying their mind. The world outside of their roundabout is surreal even in their dreams. A small spark shoots from the trident of the Priest and burns the attacking cobra to ashes.

The skeleton laughs at the precarious and helpless passengers, without even looking back to avoid the unavoidable for the living beings.

Slowly, a white ash-like powder starts falling from the sky. It is coming up to the head of the passengers in the circle and melting away. The temperature of the whole ground is falling rapidly. The white powder is nothing but snow; however, it is getting heavier every moment. First, it converts to flakes and then the flakes accumulate into big layers of snow. Within no time, the whole ground is covered with snow; the Priest has been transformed into a mound of snow. Apart from the edges of the trident, only the funeral pyre and the small circle are free from snow. The snakes have been buried in a snow grave.

Even though the snow is not able to fall inside the circle, it is still able to suck the temperature out from its whole atmosphere. The shivering bodies of the passengers are finding it difficult to keep still – a muster from the Priest. Their fingers are getting numb. The three of them are slowly crouching with each other to keep warm. Their lips are turning blue and their eyes are looking fragile.

There is something in the snow in front of the Priest. It moves towards the fire swiftly. Breach lunges out of the moving mound of snow, and when she is close enough to the skeleton, she snatches the blue stone from it and flies over the fire to land right in front of the circle. She drops the stone inside the circle and returns to her place in front of the Priest. The mere presence of the stone raises the temperature of the circle immediately.

A missile made of burning wood shoots out from the funeral pyre towards Breach; right at that moment, a shooting star comes out of nowhere from the sky and intercepts the missile before it can hit the canine.

So accurate and closely knit are the patterns of this world. A star that broke millions of years ago was destined to this particular miniscule moment to save Breach. Nothing in this world is random; each and every thing, every moment is defined to serve, every action is defined to collaborate.

The collision of the star with earth was enough to break the spell of snow and melt it. The melting snow brings the thought of thirst to the passengers' parched mouths. Fear or desire, the mind's space never remains on one thing.

"Before I can answer your unknown question, I have something to learn from you," the Priest presents a request to the burning dead.

"Go ahead!" The infuriated fire screams at him.

"How does the corporal world and life look from the state you are in right now?"

"What if I don't answer?"

"You are my guru, before I be yours, which will be shortly," the Priest is not amused at the bantering.

"What does your Adrushya Guru say?" The ghost attempts to further deflect the question.

"He says to experience it rather than to hear it," The Priest replies.

"So, do it!" The ghost is irritated now.

"I can do it now, but what about you? Do you want to remain as the half-burnt demon you are here?" Now is the time for the Priest to smile. His eyes are still furious.

The dead man stands up from the pyre bed and starts walking towards the circle – the passengers' limited world.

"Don't even think about it!" The Priest shouts out; his voice has a threatening power as well as the helplessness of not being able to do anything should the ghost decide to take any extreme step.

"Don't worry, I am not at that state yet, I know I need an answer and I also know that you belong to the world of bondages, not me," the skeleton assures the Priest as it stares at the group.

A mere look from this ghost/dead man/skeleton is so chilling, that it is enough for all three to start feeling a cold sweat dripping from their foreheads. Their hearts are pumping violently to avoid this stare and run away to the composed stream of Ganga. It is struggling like a wild bird in a cage.

"Why are you people worried about becoming extinct?" It asks while standing at the edge of the circle and looking at them intensely.

"Do not answer, do not move!" The Priest interrupts before the girl lets anything out of her half-open lips.

"Ha-ha! That's what he wants to know and now he doesn't want your erudite people to answer," The ghost replies itself.

It strolls around the circle while voraciously looking at them.

"OK, I will answer your question, but in return, you will answer

157

mine and also, I need one of the passengers to accompany me," The ghost adds a condition.

"What if we refuse this condition?" The Priest shoots back at him.

"Well, when I say: 'I am leaving', it is in the context of language you people understand, but not what the actual words mean!" The skeleton/ghost clarifies. "I am going to become omniscient and omnipresent, and therefore will not actually be 'leaving', but instead, become able to do 'anything' beyond limited human standards. So, either one of you will accompany me, or all of you, it's your choice; no other option"

The blazing skeleton turns back, leaving a trail of fire, ashes and dripping molten flesh around the circle and walks towards the pyre.

"The state where I am, most of the world and living beings look like a bunch of stupid, senseless nomads, most of them don't know what they are trying to achieve and they just keep on dying repeatedly – being born again and again and again; you are living an empty life and dying an incomplete death.

There are very few souls, who are actually utilizing their reason of existence and who will succeed in one life or another.

And what a funny way to create excuses in order to avoid the inevitable; you guys have defined unlimited boundaries for yourself, such as: nothing can move faster than light; if you don't sleep than you are going to die; if you don't eat then our body will become week and so on and so on!

What they try to avoid are two simple things: death and truth." It sits down on the fire-bed again.

The truth is inevitable; so is the death, but the latter cannot be complete until truth is realized. Every one of us at birth has the simplest thing in this world to do, and that is to realize our truth. However, the cycle of nature is like a game. Just after birth, when we know the truth, we do not have the power to realize it. Then once we get the power to act, we do not have courage to realize it, and once we get courage to act, we don't have truth to realize, and in the end, when we again get to it, we lose power, courage and truth itself to death, making it all a useless effort, and a waste of opportunity.

This cycle keeps running like an infinite game and we keep on struggling in one phase or another.

Fortunately, I realized my truth in my first ever birth. My quest to get the answer of my question was my truth.

Up here where I am standing right now, it is kind of a middle ground: a transient state. I know I must achieve my truth to realize a sensible death, to complete my cycle of deaths. At this stage, I can clearly see the difference between the two sides.

This world is bound in mind, space, and time; it is defined by past, present, and future without providing a link between them. This is a spatial continuous movement of the world and life as opposed to the absolute still consciousness of my new abode."

In the new world, future is the past of the present. There is no difference of space and time; there is an ultimate inertia applied to the supreme awareness because there is no boundary.

We feel the need of time and space in this physical world because we define boundaries at every level. Once boundaries are defined; there comes the need of correlation between these boundaries and then the differences. Subsequently come the light, darkness and other adjectives.

The other world is simply devoid of light and darkness, day and night, it does not follow the slavery of any adjectives. There is no one proving oneself to others, because no one is better than anybody else is. In fact, there is nothing as 'anybody', or I should say there is 'nobody'. It is a collective one supreme consciousness. You can reach everywhere at any point of time and space in this world. You can even witness this physical world and laugh out at the stupidity of these innocent centers of the universe."

"Looks impossible?" He turns around and looks at the problematic faces of the passengers. "Seems like a joke?"

"Do not respond! It knows the truth," the Priest stalls the initiation of conversation with the ineligibles. "If you respond, it will have more questions for you, and if you don't answer it will have the right to do what it is best at."

"Yes, I know the truth, I can say you are in the right direction, kill the tigers and meet with the ocean, it will take you to your destination in desert, or tell me to finish your job and join me in the next world!" The dead man looks ferociously at the Priest." Still, if you want to carry the burden of it for yourself, go ahead."

"But, let's be very clear – Jesus did walk on water. He did cure the incurables. Mohammad did read the book from the sky on the table of the consciousness, and descended it for human beings to follow. Krishna did show the Chidakasha – his omnipresent and eternal form to Arjun, who had the eligible eyes to look. Even you can do this; nothing and no one except your self-imposed limits, can stop you. I admit I had to break this spell of confinement eleven times to reach this point, but it was only in my first attempt, when I had to initiate myself, the rest all happened automatically.

Recall your calls for help to your mother in your childhood. She would make sure that she found you no matter where you were. No matter how much time it might have taken to find you, but she would be there right in time," the dead man is calm again and the conversation continues. "There is no God or Gods for the dead because God is associated with qualities and no qualities are required for what is already the universal itself.

I am Allah and Allah is I. All Krishna said is what I told him that he taught me. I was crucified as Christ, and the ultimate consciousness bled along with me. At the same time, the power of this consciousness resurrected him from death, just because he was following his quest.

This is the only limited description in the finite capacity of worldly languages that I can provide you at this point. And, this limitation is for two reasons: one, your brain, shackled by the rules of this world, will not be able to accept a more 'truthful' and complete description and secondly, it cannot be told in words but must be experienced, as your Adrushya Guru rightly said. There were very few people like Mohammad, sages of ancient time, Jesus for example, who got a glimpse of this consciousness, and then there was nothing impossible for them in this mortal world.

What makes these two worlds different – The ego. Death in itself is not the reason for fear, but the ego is. It is our ego, which rightly gets afraid, because it loses its identity upon death.

Death is not an escape of the soul into the sky; it is actually a dissipation of the ego to become Adrushya Guru, to become infinite. It is the dissociation of energy and consciousness; the dissolution of the identity of energy, converting itself from the individual person, to universal consciousness.

When we are born, there is a universal dynamic energy that seeds the concept of space and time in the form of life. Once these seeds are destroyed by supreme knowledge, desires diminish, and the expansion of time and space stops. The original dynamic energy subdues, resulting in the contraction of time and space. It shrinks back to the infinite within the zero. It unravels the mystery. It opens the gateway to the infinite.

When a person dies, the soul does not go anywhere outside of the body to the heavens. Actually, his or her ego collapses in the energy. It is like Kaali standing on the Mahakala – The great conqueror of death – Shiva; resulting in its manifestation of the universal consciousness.

That is why human beings either burn or bury their loved ones. By burning the body, time and space of the body evaporates, without leaving a trace of the soul. By burying, we make the body one with earth; again, it doesn't leave a trace for the soul to look back at its mortal confinement."

The skeleton ghost turns around and looks at the passengers.

"And for some, it may be the answer to why one's most loved one is responsible for initiating the holy fire or throwing the first grains of earth on the grave." – It is hinting this answer to Bhaijan's question of why a son must torch his own parent's funeral pyre.

"The simple lesson is to not bind yourself in any limitations, find your true self, and unleash it from the chains of rules and rationality. Stop judging. Moreover, start EXPERIENCING!

And, that's where the answer to your question completes and my question starts."

———————————◆ ◆ ◆ ◆ ◆ ◆———————————

The dead man's eyes shed some lava like tears at this point. "What is the objective of achieving our Goal? What does the universal soul achieve after the journey is complete? Why does it put its own part into these seemingly useless cycles?" It asks while slowly leaning on the burning wood sticks.

The outer part of its body is already becoming ash now, resulting in a faded white shape of a human being. The mortal body is at its core with hardly any indication of the gender of the living being. The fire is also burning with higher and more sporadic flames, as it does just before dying out.

The Priest's eyes are closed and his face shows that he is in deep meditation. It has been almost twelve hours since he moved even an inch from the place where he has been standing. The sun is still not out, but birds have started to sing their morning raga, something that was missing the previous evening.

Everybody on the ground is looking at him; they are waiting to hear the response.

The dead man turns around and looks at the passengers, and suddenly.... they forget all the good things about death – It is still their enemy number one. The live bodies start sweating, the wounds are forgotten, and the only ray of hope that the Priest is watching them is already gone, as he is deep in his thoughts to find the answer for the dead man.

"Do you know science?" The Priest's voice breaks the tussle and diverts the attention of the hunter as well as the game.

"Haa! Which science are you talking about, yours or mine?" The dead man laughs off the question. "You don't even have 'science'; your so-called science is nothing but a way to say how things happen. It never says why things happen the way they occur at all. It puts numerous limits on actual science. No matter how far it goes in space, how deep it goes into an atom, it always tries to find a shape or form and confines itself into those boundaries."

"So, what's your science?" The Priest asks him.

"Don't you know?"

"Help me to understand it."

"Very simple, it is the science to be still but not dynamic; to be silent but not a sound, to be infinite but not relative. In a single word – it is nothing but truth. It is the logic of being absolute and detached," The skeleton's eyeholes chuckle with excitement. "Try to follow this science to see how the time and space created by our minds falls apart, and opens the gates of infinite possibilities."

"So, before knowing what the goal of life is, we need to know what life itself is, even though you haven't asked for it, I am going to tell you, as you favored me by answering my question so beautifully," the Priest admires the dead man now, "I have to be completely honest with you and myself today. I was looking for the answer of what death is, and what the purpose of the death is. Actually, I was afraid of it, even though I have literally been breathing and sleeping with the dead, day and night"

The passengers look a bit relaxed, as the redness of the dead man has become less intense now. The fire had become almost like a simple pile of hot pieces of coal. The girl remaining true to her character opens her mouth and tries to interject her opinion into the conversation.

"Don't say a word! I have been warning you since the night of life started unfolding. I do not care if you die, but if you do, you will leave your body without realizing your goal, and I do not want to carry that burden with my soul and return to this mortal dream again. I have the choice of nothing and everything, and I want to return to this nothingness," Aghori's eyes are now scarier even than those of the dead man. "You are safe inside the circle with your limited knowledge and enjoying this experience as the fantasy. If you dare to venture out into the kingdom of truth, be ready to face it the way it is; in your mortal words: it is brutal. I can assure you that you are safe inside the periphery in your physical appearance. However, you cannot control your voice to not travel outside of it. Once it comes out of the circle, nothing can escape the truth. It is like a black hole and the dead man is the one standing at the center of it; don't think it is just a burning pile of bones, converting to ashes!"

The self-content elderly man, listening to what he already knows smiles back at the rebuttal.

"Listen to it. Apply it to your path and carry on to achieve your goal. Like that meteorite: it had everything planned very well here, like a train, that you board daily to go to work; one is scheduled by you and the other by your universal consciousness," the Priest concludes his point but the dead man does not like it.

"I thought you were going to answer my question, weren't you?" It says with weary anger in its eyes.

"I beg your pardon, but I have my mortal duty to conduct, which is equally as important as the one I am doing for you right now," the Priest replies while apologizing to the dead man.

"So, let's start with life; what is life? Is it real? How did it materialize? Then we will logically come to the point where you will get the answer to your question – what is the purpose of life – the goal of all goals in our life.

Life is nothing, but a thought sparked out the infinite by the super consciousness. This thought is the God for life. As soon as this thought triggers, it follows its own course of existence. It creates its own universe. No one but our own thoughts create the whole world around us. Nothing exists for me if I cease to exist. Similarly, nothing will be there if you are not there to perceive it.

You, as a thought, occur, then you see your light, and when light appears, darkness follows, then, follows God – Generator, Operator and Destroyer – input, process and output – holy son, father and ghost. It is now, when thought feels the sense of being powerful. It is where consciousness plays the game with it. It gives birth to the Ego. Subsequently, ego takes control and starts building its own complicated world. Although it wants to be king of this world, it still has to have the thought to be there. Ego cannot allow thought to go back to nothingness.

What is the best way to keep your most valuable possession in the world?" The Priest asks.

"When I was alive, I used to do it by locking it in a safe place," The dead man replies like a child.

"Exactly, and you make sure that the safe place is built in such a way that no one can access it without your knowledge. Similarly, this is what our ego does: it starts creating a safe place by imposing a new world, rules, and constraints on the original thought. It starts building this illusion around it: childhood, toys, relationships, emotions, education, true-false, day-night, stories, books, entertainment, health and so on and so on. Ego brings so many puzzles around the thought that it forgets to be creative. Ego is also creating, you may argue, but those creations are purposefully relative. It buries the ultimate conception inside those elusive creations."

The Priest looks up at the deep sky. For some strange reason, the sky feels a bit closer to the ground. He continues with his explanation, "this whole life is a big drama. Ego has set it up to survive as long as it can, even though it knows that it is going to lose the drama one day. The balloon it is pumping up, will inflate one day in no time. Anything and everything that is created will be destroyed one day sooner or later; except the original thought."

"Then why are we even born to have an objective in our life? Why are there others born to serve so called humanity?" The dead man asks.

"As I told you earlier, we are not born, it's a thought that sparked and made an ego for itself; there is no one 'born', but a thought that ignited and created an entire world around it. It does what it is best at," the Priest clarifies. "There is no one, and nothing, existing in this world; not even a small stone, or the invisible air or even the infinite sky, but you. It's your thought's manifestation that I am standing in front of you, challenging you, and at the same time a few people are sitting behind you, scared of you."

"You mean there is no one around me; nothing at all, just my imagination?" The diminishing fire in the dead body lights up again due to curiosity. Some of the old ash flies away in the wind, creating a hallucinating scene of an expanding body, which then blows up into pieces before the actual and shorter one with fresh ash skin is visible.

"Exactly, there is nothing. How can you have anything out of nothing?" The Priest justifies. "Even this world's science cannot define that. For, they always define that if there is anything then it should be inside the boundary, and if there is a boundary then, there must be another limit overlying that boundary. It goes until infinity; and infinity is what? Nothing, Science cannot define it.

Your science, the cosmic knowledge proves it is in everything. Be still, be absolute, and when you are absolute then there is nothing but you; who in yourself is nothing."

"So, what is it that I am seeing around me, and also what others who are living in this world are seeing, observing and experiencing; things that I didn't even know as a human being?" The ghost asks.

"Just a while ago when you were my Guru, you said that the future is the past of the present in the conscious world," the Priest enquires as a teacher does to his students. "What does that mean? What does time and space mean?"

He pauses but does not wait for an answer; the same is the case with the dead man; it is not even trying to answer, but being more attentive with its shrinking body to listen to the Priest.

"Past, present and future are nothing but the quality of the time: past is realized; present is the current experience; and future is the goal.

Ego is the seed of the past, consciousness is the element of the present, and the future is the arena of war between ego and thought.

Time is relative to space, which is nothing but manifestation of the ego," the Priest concludes one part of his answer.

"I am confused; are you saying if I don't exist nothing else exists?" The dead man asks.

"Umhmm; you had experienced some of the things during your mortal childhood that were simply part of the fantasy, and by the time you grew up, those same things become reality for the masses, didn't they?" The Priest confirms the experience.

"Then how does thought appear; and from where does it appear; and what is the purpose for the thought to appear?" The ghost is still looking for clarifications, "I am more familiar with death, so I told you about that and what follows, but not about the past of this future."

"Haha," the Priest smiles at him. "So, you know where are you heading to, but not where you have just come from? What is your ultimate state, where time and space is just one wrapper for you?"

"If I would have known it, I wouldn't have needed you to answer, which as per you is nothing but me only, defining in a different way," the dead man replies to the Priest.

"Not you, but your ego has created me. The answer was actually required by your thought which gave me the power to think and help you," the Priest replies.

"So how does thought appear; and from where does it appear; and what is the purpose of it? I don't have answer to that. Moreover, why does it even matter to know that; do not be the 'science' of ignorance or boundaries.

The science of this mortal world asks a question and needs an answer – with proof. If it does not see proof, it simply declares it as false.

What is it best at? It simply defines 'how' something happens, not the 'why' of that phenomenon happening.

No one knows why the earth revolves around the Sun; why galaxies exist; why there are days and nights; why we define right and wrong in this world; why the big bang happened.

The answer to the second part of your question lies in this simple word –Why!

Why do we have a goal in our life? The answer is even simpler than the question itself." The whole area shakes up as the Priest releases his pose with the landing of his second foot on the ground.

"Just to conquer our ego," he concludes.

"This simple statement defines the actual common goal of our lives."

The dead man is almost a frame of ash now with the funeral pyre completely quelled. The remains of the burning dead body walk towards the Priest, who opens his arms to receive the dead with a warm heart.

Breach moves out of the way and lunges towards the circle of mortal life – the small world in which we live in. The Priest and the dead man hug each other and both slowly convert into ashes showering down from the clear sky. The dawn is at its peak. The land slowly becomes lush green. Birds are chirping again. The earth is still revolving, and now the passengers know why it does – It is conspiring for them to overthrow their ego. Ganga is still flowing to quench the thirst of millions.

The girl and Bhaijan rush towards the pile of the ash remains. They are crying at the loss of the Priest; their battle with the ego is still going on.

The elderly man gently walks towards them and smiles at their fresh ignorance. "I don't know whether you belong to my drama or I am part of yours. Nevertheless, what I do know is that we must not get trapped by our ego. We received enlightenment today. Let us not waste this power. Let us move towards our goal."

Bhaijan collects the ashes in the long corner of his shirt with the girl and elderly man's help.

Breach is busy playing with the blue stone left by them, having been distracted by the witnessing of the departure of Aghori's soul. Perhaps, the stone was not part of the drama between the dead disciple and deadly mentor. It may, however, have some role to play in the future.

They close one chapter of the novel written by their ego and get ready to turn the page to the next nameless world. Clearly, by the time the sun's fresh ray fall on their faces, their attitude has changed towards their own existence.

sahasrara

(THE SELFLESS PURITY)

--- SAHASRARA ---
(THE SELFLESS PURITY)

Silence is the main speaker again. All the passengers have boarded the boat. Bhaijan starts navigating, and the others just lie down on the floor, looking at the sky. There are many storms raging in their minds.

The boat passes by a shallow patch before merging into another bigger artery. Bhaijan puts the boat in the middle of the stream and closes his eyes. Breach is standing at the front as a pallbearer and guide of the boat with an unknown sailor at the helm.

Everyone is trying to find their original script, written by the ego. They want to pick it out, and change it but are not able to find the required pages. The ego is proving to be a shrewder entity then they thought. It is equipped with the knowledge of what is coming ahead.

One good thing, however, is that the boat does not have an ego and it knows the best thing it can do is – to follow the stream.

They are sailing in the river Padma now, their boat crosses into Bangladesh without any issues. The passengers are oblivious to hunger, or other physical desire. They are just lying on the floor. Someone is sleeping with their eyes open, and others are awake with closed eyes. Their ego is fighting a lost battle.

Their first stop is in a small town called Kushtia on the bank of river Padma, a tributary of Ganga.

"Welcome to the origin of the non-violent revolution of India, the mother of the Satyagraha of Gandhi!" The elderly man breaks the silence after almost three days of travelling towards an unspecified destination.

"Wait, Satyagraha by Gandhi was done in Gujarat, not here in the east," Bhaijan retracts himself to the mortal world.

"True, I said Mother of Satyagraha was born here, not Satyagraha itself," the elderly man clarifies. "The Indigo revolution of Nadia and Khulna was the first non-violent protest against the industrialists and the greediest of the British Empire. This was the first ever incident in human history when endurance converted resistance. It became an inspiration for Gandhi to start Satyagraha."

"Did Gandhi exist?" The girl is still looking at things through the lens of that epic night.

"Maybe, or maybe not. Maybe he is a character of our own theatre; but how does it matter?" The elderly man replies. "Even this town, the boat, and the revolutions are nothing but some of the chapters out of the book of duals between our ego and consciousness."

"I have changed my whole thought process since that night of origination of the new universe in myself," the girl says.

"It's good to do that but remember we haven't yet reached our goal so we need to continue the voyage. The day we reach our destination, everything will be alright," the elderly man persuades her to be in the world created by her instead of leaving it abruptly, and missing the goal.

They replenish their supplies in the town and leave after a brief stop there. The locals, who generally help smugglers and fugitives to cross over the border and disappear in the wilderness of Bangladesh, guide them to follow the next stream, called River Madhumati.

Another three days of floating and sailing brings them to the border of Sundarban – the world's largest cluster of deltas. AntarMauna – the inner silence, the science of the other world, is the new way of living on the boat now. The conversation has remained subtle, until one day, when Bhaijan restarts their game from where it was left off just before the ghostly night when they lost their Priest friend.

———————— ◆ ◆ ◆ ◆ ◆ ————————

"It was the Priest's turn to speak about himself and he did speak on that night with the dead man. However, he only revealed about his goal, not about his experience," Bhaijan breaks the silence about the mysterious Priest. "The Priest belonged to an ultra-rich family of Banaras town. His mother was the sole heir of a small kingdom nearby Banaras. At his personal capacity, he was one of the most prominent scientists at CERN. His core expertise was in explaining the science in the Vedas and exploring the application of those solutions in the Great Experiment. One day he received news that his only relative in this world – his mother, had passed away. Although he was dejected, he still put his work ahead of his personal priorities. He got five days off to come back and complete the final rites of his mother. Unfortunately, by that time, her body was already decaying and his brother conducted the final rites to usurp the royal estate.

As usual, the way you have seen there in Banaras, his mother's partially charred body was left floating in Ganga by the so-called professional caretakers. He came back to Banaras and faced humiliation, not only from his brother but also from other relatives as well.

That was the best day of my life, when he came to me and requested that I take him to the farthest corners of the river. Considering him a customer with deep pockets, I took him to the same island where you saw the mass cremation done by us. He found his mother's half-burnt and decaying body stuck in the marsh. It was an earth shattering moment for him. He completely broke down after finding her corpse. He remained on that uninhabited island with his mother's body for two days. Somehow, I couldn't leave him crying and mourning for his mother.

Finally, I persuaded him to let it go. We did her last rites once again but he still refused to leave the island. I returned to my house. However, I couldn't forget him. The island became a second home to me. Somehow, I felt compelled, by myself to arrange all the necessities for him. Once a filthy rich prince, he was one of the poorest persons in my eyes now.

Even Prophet Muhammad has said: it is mother, who is the most adorable and venerable to him in this world; she is beyond anything, even father. Days and weeks passed, but he didn't move an inch from the island, as if he was waiting for someone there.

One day an Aghori asked me to see him. They became master and disciple. I got the privilege of learning the science behind Aghorism; learning English from the Pundit became by-product of that experience.

After his master left the island, he dedicated himself to cleaning Ganga and making sure that all the bodies were disposed of properly. We used to get five Rupees for the disposal of each body. He was happy with this because he was more interested in his self-satisfaction rather than money.

Slowly people who used to mock us, and tried to break our friendship started adopting us. They accepted us as part of their reason for existence. For them we were unavoidable, we were like the vultures who kept their backyard clean.

What an interesting human trait, if you are falling down a path, there will be people who will hold you and support you. At the same time, these very people can be the biggest and toughest obstacles when you try to rise above them. The Pundit used to call it an 'induction effect' as in science. Always be in your equilibrium with other people. If you try to break it, there will be resistance.

The Pundit used to have dreams and I used to interpret them for him. For quite a while, the Pundit was dreaming about this castle, you and Breach. He was so clear about you and Breach, that he made multiple sketches of, and perhaps kept them with himself while waiting for you to arrive."

As soon as they enter in Sundarban, Bhaijan switches off the boat, but it continues to sail fast due to strong currents in the river. The changing course of the river is clearly visible on the banks. It is just after a heavy rain and people are busy setting up their huts on the new lands.

The elderly man asks Bhaijan to stop at a small island and asks Joan to hide in the cabin. Bhaijan docks the boat and both of them go in a small hut to meet some strangers.

It doesn't take much time for them to return excitedly. They have found a person who can take her to the embassy tomorrow morning. Now they have to wait in the shanty for the night.

But to Joan's surprise, US citizens are too precious to let go from the common gangsters' hands around the world. Within no time, their identity is revealed to the thugs. Joan is incarcerated in the boat with no signs of Bhaijan or the elderly man. She doesn't take it offensively. She considers it as her destiny, but her egoist instinct is back, and start pushing her to find Andrew. It is still not defeated.

"Where is he? How can I find him? Is he still even alive?" are the thoughts rolling around in her mind. Her ego is once again, trying to build the new world around her and dragging her back to its arena. Now she knows it is almost impossible to go to the embassy, she doesn't even know where in the world she is imprisoned.

Sometimes when things seemingly get out of control, we should become water. Keep flowing with the time, and then there will be rocks and there will be forests, there will be high cliffs too; just keep on conquering them, steadily and silently. Because, these are the obstacles we need to overcome to meet the confluence – to overcome the drama of the ego.

Wait for the right time to hit your ego quietly and precisely. Wait for the right place to quench the thirst of it. Until then, keep on flowing, slowly, steadily, and silently. For, the path to your destination will become very clear someday. It is inevitable that the ego will lose its fight on that day. Nevertheless, it is equally important to watch the victory from your own eyes.

Do not forget to carry a plank and stones with you, because they are nothing but experiences. They are the lessons that will be useful to you at right time. This is exactly what Joan is waiting for, the next step by the traffickers, so that she can forge a path for her known journey, with unknown destination.

The day arrives; again, destiny has the toughest lessons lined up for Joan to learn, so that she is ready for her final test. She is shifted to a small hut in the delta to shoot a ransom video.

It is raining heavily when a fight ensues between smugglers and the pimps from Banaras who have been chasing Joan since she left the brothel. A pack of Bengal tigers attacks the camp at the same time. Joan, in spite of giving a hard fight to both the gangs and tigers, is seriously injured. She is lying on the grass and seeing a faded image of the elderly man, fighting with the only tiger left alive on the ground.

"Go away!" She is hearing a fading shout from the elderly man while he struggles to overcome the tiger's attack.

Breach is confused, at one moment, she is trying to drag Joan away, and at the other, she is helping the elderly man fend off the tiger. Joan is in a ghostly state, in which she is present all around. She can see Bhaijan lying unconscious inside the cabin in the boat. One eye of the elderly man is hanging out of his skull. His stomach is clearly spilling out of his body. However, he is still smiling.

"I used to dream of fighting with tigers. That dream has come true today," the elderly man is holding the tiger with his hand right in its mouth. "Today this dream is fulfilled. You are moving in the right direction towards your goal, just follow it along."

The girl is struggling to say something but she can't. She is witnessing a bloody fight where the elderly man is losing on physical grounds, but is far more victorious in his own world. The selfless world where everyone is working for another is dominating the air at this moment.

"Go, your goal is waiting for you eagerly. You don't have much time in this world," the elderly man picks the tiger up in the air and bangs it on the ground to sit on it. The blood dripping from his stomach is falling right into the mouth of the tiger. The elderly man is severely injured, but its tiger that is losing the battle.

She is moving away from the scene. She is out of her body and seeing herself lying on the ground. "Remember, you are nothing and everything if you leave the body. The only door to reach the ultimate path is through the body, not outside of the body," the elderly man is sitting calmly on top of the helpless tiger. "Don't forget to carry it until you reach there. It will automatically be recycled at the right time."

The girl blinks and finds herself back in worldly constraints. She is feeling the pain; her body is not able to get up and the elderly man is almost dead with the tiger sitting on top of him now. She is confused about which world is her reality. She knows she has only limited time to go back to the boat and sail away.

Breach is helping her get on her feet. She agonizingly crawls towards the boat. It takes ages for her to cover some fifty meters of muddy patch. The only thing working in her favor is that the tiger is busy feasting on the elderly man. It is eating with a sense of pride that it has conquered its worst enemy, a human.

Finally, the girl is on the boat, collapsing back into the darkness within her, the other form of reality. Breach pushes the boat from the bank to the main stream. It is getting darker and the boat starts to float steadily and slowly along with the current towards the unknown.

The boat is very much like a heavily used pen that carries the writing pattern of the owner. Who says that non-living things do not have any consciousness? Alternatively, I must ask: who says that there is anything that is 'non-living' in this universe?

———— ✦ ✦✦✦✦ ✦ ————

A hollow tin-box like object and some stones are making noises on the boat's deck. It is a bright and humid day; the boat is dwindling and frolicking into the waves that are just being playful and not dangerous to be a storm.

The girl wakes up as Breach licks off flies and germs from her wounds. Their boat is in the middle of nowhere. They have drifted out into the Bay of Bengal.

She is unable to move due to the injuries she sustained in the fight. It was only her courage, if not Breach, that had pushed her inside the boat to look at another sunrise.

She stares at the sky; deep, blue and infinite. Sometimes her body shakes due to tides in the ocean. Breach is wandering around her. She keeps licking her wounds to protect from the flies that are coming out of the cabin.

She remains lying standstill as days and nights pass by, until one fine day, when she senses that there is someone else on the boat. Her dehydrated body doesn't deter her happiness to be physically alive. She has gone through similar experiences earlier in her life, so she knows the value of being alive; she understands what matters in such situation very well.

In the silence of the water desert, her doubt about any company on the boat is not unfounded. She can hear someone making slow and painful grumbles from inside the cabin. All of a sudden, she has the relativity, and relativity brings with it uncertainty, which in turn converts to fear – a healthy ingredient for the ego to fiddle around with duality.

"Who is that? Is it a tiger? No, it cannot be, otherwise I would have been its food by now; why would it wait behind half-opened doors. Is it Bhaijan? The elderly man? Or yet another ghost who missed out to tell me about his or her experiences and goals of life?"

Thoughts and imagination are the only things she is able to move around for herself – for better or worse. She keeps on thinking and the mysterious sound keeps on growing. One thing is for sure, although she has enormous physical pain in her body, she is still feeling composed on a psychological level as no one has hurt her psychologically for so long. The physical brutality is much easy to bear than any psychic cruelty.

It's the sixth day since she has gained her consciousness back. Still, in spite of having no water or food, she is able to start moving her hands and feet. Maybe, she has lost enough weight to pick herself up with her remaining strength.

It is a sudden restart of life for her. The timely rain not only gives her respite from the humidity, but also enough water to drink so that she feels energized from the inside. She slowly drags herself to the sidewall of the boat and leans on it. It used to be the favorite spot for the Priest to come and sit during their journey. Breach is by her side as always, and on the other side is the skull, full of water with the blue stone inside it.

Suddenly there is a big sound as if someone is trying to cut something with a heavy dagger inside the cabin.

Breach lunges inside the cabin; strangely, she is not attacking anyone, but excitedly meeting someone close. She comes back with a loaf of meat in her jaw; her tail is wagging after visiting the cabin.

The loaf of meat turns out to be one of the most unbelievable things falling from the sky for the girl. The last thing she was expecting to come out of cabin was the food. Until now, she was waiting to starve to her destiny – death. She is so weak that it takes her two minutes to grab the piece of meat and take a bite of it. It tastes different but that hardly matters to her. At this moment, she is like an animal, like a baby who can eat anything and everything. Its after a couple of bites that she realizes that she is eating nothing but human flesh. She wants to throw it out but she cannot. Her body needs some food at this time and that is more important than what is right or wrong as per her social learnings. She abhorrently eats the precious loaf of human meat.

Her mind starts flying again, thanks to the nourishment of food. Her ego is bringing in the uncertainties of living. The certainty of dying has diminished a little with few mouthfuls of human flesh.

She gathers her nerves to start crawling towards the cabin. Her curiosity about the strange voices coming from inside the cabin is irresistible now. It takes her three hours to crawl the ten feet of distance from the edge of the boat to the door of the cabin.

The moment she peeks inside the cabin, her sky topples down on the boat. It is Bhaijan, lying in one corner of the cabin, with a machete in one hand. A decomposing corpse of a huge man is lying on him. He has dried blood all around his face and on his clothes. It is clear from the scene inside the cabin that Bhaijan was inside the cabin when attacked, perhaps he overpowered this giant attacker but at the cost of some irreparable injuries inflicted on him.

Bhaijan is asleep with a peaceful face like that of a sleeping baby. The girl, with tears of joy and pain together in her eyes, slowly inches towards him. As she approaches Bhaijan, he picks up and swings the machete to defend himself. The flying machete pumps adrenaline in her body, resulting in her jumping to her feet to get away from the arch of the edge. The girl is standing on her feet now! After almost three weeks of stillness, she is able to move. To her surprise, for all these days she was just not attempting to stand up on her own. She was imagining that her legs were disabled and didn't have enough strength to bear her weight. Her mind starts reminiscing about the earlier conversations with her beloved stranger friends. The day, when she jumped in the water and learnt how to swim, is flashing in front of her eyes. She is once again learning the power of attempting without the assumptions of weakness and impossibilities.

Bhaijan opens his eyes to find the girl standing in front of him. He is elated and crying with joy but cannot speak. The girl discovers soon enough that the tongue in his mouth is missing with shattered jaw. His body is disabled except one of his hands with the other one severely fractured. His legs are twisted towards the back in a very awkward position.

The girl jumps on Bhaijan and gives him a very warm and tight hug. Both of them are crying. Their union is that of two souls with just one relation – they are one. There is no distinction between the two. There is no relativity. It feels like ages have passed before the girl releases Bhaijan. She realizes there is no water in the cabin. The dried lips of Bhaijan reveal the thirst he has been bearing for so many days. She runs outside with her awkwardly moving feet. The skull-bowl is still full of water. She picks it up and carefully returns to Bhaijan. Every drop in it is precious. Sometimes nature puts us in peculiar situations – Even in the middle of ocean, people can be at the verge of dying of thirst. Abundance has no significance if we can't use it properly at the right time.

Bhaijan has great difficulty drinking without a tongue but he needed the water badly. The glow of his eyes changes as soon as some water enters his throat, there is a new life in them. He is crying now but cannot express whether the tears are of pain or sorrow or even happiness. The girl joins him in shedding tears.

She painfully pulls the decomposing body off of Bhaijan's feet and drags him out of the bloody mess around him with the help of Breach. It is the very first time Bhaijan is coming out of the cabin since they left Sundarban. In fact, he cannot even believe that they escaped Sundarban alive. The bright sunshine in the middle of the Indian Ocean is too much light for him after such a long dark period inside the cabin. Nevertheless, he is happy now, not just because he is seeing the light and is still alive, but also because he has Joan with him, and she is alive too.

Joan realizes that Bhaijan's legs are rotting, and he does not have much time to survive if they are left untreated.

"You are going to die," she tells Bhaijan upfront while holding in her tears, "Really? Do you still believe in death, are you still scared of it? Even after such an incredible journey through the Ganga?" Comes the self-argument from herself.

"Really, do you still believe in death, are you still scared of it? Even after such an incredible journey through the Ganga?" Bhaijan replies while looking at the distance with water all around. He does not feel pain because he doesn't have any sense either in his body or in his soul; his body is injured beyond any possibilities to repair, and his soul is inert to any materialistic sense now. He is simply smiling with only few remaining teeth and no tongue to show.

Sometimes when we see others in more pain than us, we start feeling stronger. Such is the situation with the girl, who was not even able to move her fingers properly a little while ago, but is now walking all over the boat. She has switched on the boat's engine and is now taking care of a patient who is in worse condition than her.

She cooks a fresh fish caught by Breach, truly no knowledge is waste in this world be it even acquired by an animal. They don't have the luxury to stop at a random island and cook food while sitting around a pit-fire. It has almost been three weeks since they had any proper food. Bhaijan vomits out all the food within no time, with lots of blood coming out with it; his situation is getting worse by the hour.

The girl is unsure what to do. She tries to pull Bhaijan inside but he refuses. He remains on the deck and they spend the whole night there under the open sky.

Thanks to their good fortune, there is no storm rising on the horizon; or may be the girl's ego is so busy with the storm within, that it simply doesn't need another one outside for the time being.

It is very early in the morning, when the sky is just turning red that someone shakes up Joan. She wakes up to see a familiar shadow running towards the cabin. She is not able to react quickly as Bhaijan is sleeping with his head on her lap. At this moment, there is nothing more important than the tranquility on Bhaijan's face. She knows there is no one else on the boat and Breach is there to protect her in case there is any danger. Perhaps she believes in Breach more than her own breath now.

She has her eyes open and can clearly see the shadow moving around inside the cabin. Slowly the shadow converts into a glow and then the glow converts into an intense light.

"Who is there?" She asks whispering.

"I am you; I am your Adrushya Guru," comes the reply from the other end.

The girl has a high voltage current running through her body now. She cannot move. Her time has come to a standstill, for her everything has crashed and become stone now. She had been waiting for all these days to come face to face with her true self and now, when it is there, she is feeling that she is not yet ready for this encounter.

"What does Adrushya Guru mean?" She asks a question. "I am still struggling or perhaps not prepared to find this answer."

"How does that matter? I am a real self of yours, created by you, for yourself. If you ask me what do I mean, it implies, how do you mean?" Comes the stone-like voice from inside. "And remember, I am just for you, not for your name; a name is nothing, just one of the identities assigned to you. It is not you."

"Then, who am I?" Asks the girl.

"That's something you need to figure out yourself. I can only help you in your ultimate search, your ultimate goal."

"What is my ultimate goal?"

"To find out, who you are."

"Are you my Ego?"

"No."

"Then who are you?"

"Adrushya Guru."

"How can I save myself from my ego? How do I kill it?" The girl next asks a witty question.

"Ego is the reason for your existence in this material world; you can conquer it, humiliate it, but cannot kill it. This ego is associated with your name and you cannot live without a name in this material world. So instead of killing it, just try to dominate it, try to resist what it imposes on you as a rule, try to do what is right in your conscience," replies the shadow.

"Can you come out and show your face?" The girl changes the topic.

"I can, but what would that matter?" Confronts the shadow.

"It matters because I cannot follow a shadow," the girl retorts.

"Who is asking you to follow shadows? You have created me. I am one of your manifestations," the voice replies from inside.

"Still I want to see if I have created something significant or not," the girl is adamant about seeing the face of the invisible shadow she has created.

"You will have to promise me one thing," the shadow demands.

"What is that?"

"You will follow what I will tell you and in return I will not only show myself to you but also give life to one of the most precious things you have with you," the shadow explains.

"My most precious thing is Bhaijan," the girl clears the air, "If I have created him as well, then I am really proud of such creativity."

"Still, I will do whatever you will say, for I have no fear of death now. Ego has just gone out of my mind and my emotions are already deceased now. I am like the stone lying there at the bottom of the ocean, waiting for a wave to take it to another place where it can serve its purpose." The girl shows some emotion at the end of the statement while curling Bhaijan's hair.

"Okay, you can see who is your better creation, me or Bhaijan," the voice changes to that of the Priest right in the middle of the statement.

The Priest comes out of the shadow. He is clean shaved, looking tidy in a white suit with matching shoes and an Indian hat, pretty much like a gentleman.

The girl is awed by his reappearance and about his out of space dressing. She is clearly confused whether Bhaijan – who fed her his own flash to keep her alive, is the precious one, or the person who took out the fear of death from her mind is the actual precious one.

"Here I am, your own Aghori, Your Adrushya Guru!"

The girl is in tears now. She cannot control her emotions at such a fantastic reunion with her savior.

"How come you are alive?" She asks.

"As long as you are alive, I am here, I haven't gone anywhere," the Priest replies, "I am not dead, I am not alive, I am around you forever."

"What is going on here?" The girl shouts at him.

"You are following your goal and you need some advice, so I have to come out to guide you. You know there is one difficult but inevitable decision you need to make but your ego and mental limitations are not allowing you to do so," the Priest transforms into the elderly man while explaining the reason.

"Now why these chimerical games?" She asks.

"It is not me, but your emotions, which you said you have conquered, that are the ones playing around. It doesn't matter in which form I exist, but it does that I give you timely advice; Its 'Why' that matters, not the 'How' or 'What'."

"Then what is that advice?" The girl asks.

"It is the same as my first condition to appear in front of you," The elderly man explains.

"And that is?" The girl is eager to listen.

"Kill Bhaijan," again, he has transformed back into the Priest.

"What? How can you advise me to do such a sin?" The girl is angry.

"Sin it may be, but that's what is justified right now and that's what you want to do too, but you still don't have courage to overcome this so called defeated ego of yours," the Priest explains. He is still calm and composed without any emotions.

"And then kill myself; is that your second condition?" She retorts furiously to her own mentor, she is questioning his motives and looking very angry.

"Samdarshi, this one word is the summary of our conversation during the whole journey," the composed Priest answers succinctly. *"Samdarshi Iccha Kachu Nahi, Harash Vishad Bhay Nahi Man Mahi."*

"And what does that mean?" The girl is not letting her emotions go.

"It means – Be unbiased; do not have any expectations but fulfill them for others. Be the one who doesn't have happiness, sorrow or even fear in his or her heart," the Priest replies.

"This is the core principle of Aghora. This is the fundamental mantra to overcome ego. This is the source of eternal peace," the Priest replies further with his face glowing as the first rays of dawn fall on his face.

"And that means to kill others? Even if they are a creation of your own? I think if I am the one who manifested Bhaijan and you, then I am your mother. How dare you advise me to kill my own child?"

"I agree; you are our mother as you created us. However, would you like to see your own son dying in pain? Remember, O Mother! You have manifested, but not given birth to us, you have done it with a purpose and that purpose is almost over now. You don't need us anymore. You need to surrender to your supreme goal alone, and let everything else go. It is the right time for him to go; or else he is just a shadow of your pure but deceased ego, which will keep diverting you from your path," the Priest is talking in a firm voice. "And, as a matter of fact, we will always be here to shed light on the right path in one form or another. We may be your mortal manifestations, but we are also the sons of your supreme being; this body is nothing to us. It may matter to you to define relations, but not to us. We are here to serve; as soon as our service is over, we are destined to return to our original state - Eternity."

He converts into the great burning ghost from the island with his last statement. His eyes are burning like red coal; his body is shedding ash with the blows of the wind. His stare at the girl is still intense. "You did not ask me not to go earlier, why? Didn't I serve any purpose for you at that time?" It asks the girl.

189

"Wait, I didn't create you!" The girl shouts back.

"Yes, you did! You were the reason that I had to take birth eleven times. You were the reason that kept me burning in fire for days, if not months! You are the only reason each and every word inscribed here; it's your own quest for our destiny that things are unravelling in these pages of life."

"But you never tried to protect me. You were trying to kill all of us, instead!" The girl negates his point again.

"Did I or was that your fear who wanted to kill you? I didn't try to kill you, but I tried to kill your fear. Compare yourself on that night with what you are today. When do you think you became afraid after that night? You are standing right in front of me without any protection of a mysterious circle. The Priest is nowhere to threaten me. Because, I am the Priest, I am the Ghost, I am the elderly man!" It shouts back at girl with its heavy voice but its facial expressions are a mix of those of the Priest, the elderly man, and the actual ghost.

"You are not afraid anymore, haven't you realized this lately?" The ghost enquires.

The girl searches her memories to find one single instance when she was afraid in the last few weeks.

"Don't think but agree to what I am saying," The ghost, now converting back to the Priest, insists on his statement.

"Similarly, after living with me, you forewent your happiness, your hate. Every time I worshiped you, and touched you, even tried to feed myself from your breasts as your son, you dominated your desires," the Priest further tries to convince her. "Here is this last thing that you have in your heart, stopping you from achieving your destiny. You need to remove it from the root of your ego."

"And what's that?" The girl has laid down her resistance now and is sort of following the Priest's statements.

"I will tell you once you follow my command to let Bhaijan go, and free him out of his pain."

"But you said you will also give life to one of the most precious things in my life, didn't you?" The Girls tries to defer, as she is still struggling to conform to the Priest's seemingly brutal instructions.

"Yes, I did, let me know or I will do what is best for you," the Priest replies.

"When you know everything, then why don't you do what is best for me?" The girl gives up to the Priest's suggestion.

"So be it," the Priest says.

He picks up the blue stone from the skull and rubs it until it dries. He throws it in the sea and hints to Breach to jump in the water and fetch it back. Breach follows the instructions instantly and comes back with the stone. The Priest gives it to the girl. The stone is glowing in the sun with its color slightly changed.

"This stone has the power to do anything for you, but its power can be utilized only once. It can also help you in reaching your destination, but it will not achieve your goal for you, because that's your destiny, not that of the stone's," the Priest moves back and leans on the sidewall of the boat.

＋◆＋◆＋◆＋

Farther on the horizon some dark clouds are gathering. It looks like a mourning crowd is getting ready for a funeral procession.

"As I said, you can use it only once, so use it wisely, and when you actually need it. It will disappear in the next thirty days," the Priest further explains about the stone. "Now it is your turn to follow the order; or rather, I should say, follow what is right for you."

"Do you think it is justified?" The girl asks. She seems to be without courage to kill Bhaijan.

"What is justified? I didn't get it; remember I am your subconscious, your Adrushya Guru, I belong to the universe where diplomatic conversations and slavery of adjectives doesn't work; you need to be very clear about what you are asking for, then only you will get an unambiguous answer."

"I mean killing of our own people, do you think it is justified?" She clarifies her statement.

"What do you mean by own people? Who is your own, who is not?" The Priest questions in firm but calm voice. "I have explained earlier as well, this world is created by you, for yourself, this is a game you are playing to reach the end, to the infinite."

"I know this question came to me from one more soul way back in time, this is a story older than history itself," the Priest continues.

"The person was called Arjuna. He had the exact same question as you do. He was also trying to reach to his destiny, but the path had to be laid on the sacrifices of his beloved ones, and he did so, eventually, because, there was no other choice," Priest is in his apparition state now.

"Who is this Arjuna and what did he do?" The girl asks curiously while moving towards Bhaijan whose lips are parched and need some water.

"You were Arjuna and I, as your Adrushya Guru at that time, was named Krishna – the Supreme Being," the Priest explains.

"Arjuna was a warrior, like you. He was exiled by his own demonic egoist creations, but his soul had created me to accompany him in the darkness of this mortal world. He killed all of his elders, mentors, friends, cousins and nephews like they were his enemies. He left no one but himself and me – his purest of creations.

But initially, just before the epic war began, his ego was dragging him to the position where you are right now. He refused to fight, right in the middle of the battlefield.

He was very clear about what he wanted to achieve. Again, if you look at the worldly interpretation of what he wanted to achieve, it was nothing but a huge kingdom. But, in the purest reality, he actually conquered his own ego. He dominated all of his creations. And since he was asking me to lay the path to his goal, to guide him to his destiny without casting any doubt on my teachings; I took him until there was a new beginning – the endless. I had him to be one with me. Once the war was over, Arjuna became Krishna and Krishna became Arjuna.

It is you, it is I, it is Bhaijan, it is Breach, and it is each and every thing in this world. We just need to realize it without having any confusion in our mind."

"Tell me more about Arjuna!"

"I am not a story teller!" The Priest fumes in a rage. "This is not for entertainment, that you just listen to what I am saying and then go to sleep! Come tomorrow, you start talking to your friends about what you read, instead of speaking to yourself that what you learnt. If you think whatever I have taught until now is a mere story at leisure, then you are reading the wrong person's story. This is a fact of life, bitter it might be, rude it may feel, but this is the truth. You are having doubts in yourself. You are having doubt in me – the utmost being in you. What are you wanting to do?"

"No, I don't have doubts in you!"

"Don't lie to me at least, I am you and you are me, so lies and excuses won't work. You simply don't want to kill Bhaijan that's why you are procrastinating, admit it."

"How do I use this stone?" The girl changes the topic but her voice is a bit more determined now.

"Just make a wish and throw it on anything you want to be part of your wish. For example, if you want to be immortal, this stone can give you physical immortality, just swallow it," the Priest explains making perfect sense of what the reason is behind this sudden change of topic.

"I don't want to be immortal and then get stuck in this beautiful body and the ever-amazing world created by me. You know that I just want to achieve my goal and move forward to be one with you."

"Then you know how to use it now," the Priest smiles back at her as she moves towards the other corner of the boat.

"Be very careful, you are going to be alone without any power after you use this stone, you will have to fight and win with the help of worldly means only." He warns girl.

"I know."

She holds Bhaijan's head in her lap and pushes the magical stone inside his mouth. Bhaijan starts shivering violently after swallowing it.

The Priest is looking at both of them but he is not visible to Bhaijan.

Slowly Bhaijan's body starts recovering; his feet are moving; his fractured hand starts showing some movement. He is opening his mouth with a tongue inside it!

"Welcome back Bhaijan, for a moment," the girl greets him without any emotions.

"Shukriya. Thank you. My Adrushya Guru!" Bhaijan replies.

"I am going to kill you in the next ten minutes. I know you want to perform your last prayer by reciting the Quran. Please do so without wasting any time."

Bhaijan kisses her feet before rising on his own. He drinks some of the water from the skull and uses the remaining to perform his ablutions before prayer. The girl is looking at him as if he is a most precious monument, and she will never get a chance to visit him in her life again.

A loud Namaaz voice is coming from the deck where Bhaijan is performing his prayers.

"Why did you waste the power of stone?" The Priest enquires.

"Did I? How can you say that you can read what I am trying to do? Why don't you know the answer yourself?" The girl retaliates with a smile.

"Although I am your subconscious, I am still not completely you, there is a subtle duality that exists between you and your subconscious, otherwise I would have taken you to the end," the Priest returns the smile.

"As you said, Bhaijan is also my creativity; I felt that he wanted to perform his prayers before departing, so I decided to give him what he wished for. I think he never prayed with such a pure heart earlier; he always had grudges in his mind, a sense of vengeance, a fire of disgust for being what he is," she explains. "I just helped him to achieve his goal of life. He has no desires left but one, and that is to just pray and be one with God. Maybe there is something for me as well."

------- ✦ ✦ ✦ ✦ ✦ -------

Suddenly, the water in the ocean starts getting thicker and muddier, there are desert like hot winds blowing around. The intensity of the sun's rays is growing every moment.

They can hear the loud shout of Allah-u-Akbar coming from a distance, and it is growing louder and louder as their boat grinds slowly towards the horizon.

It takes them just the blink of an eye to find themselves standing in the middle of a desert with the Grand Mosque of Mecca right in front of them. The center of Islam – the most important pillar of Islam – is staring at them. The Priest is calm as usual, with no surprise on his face. Bhaijan is facing towards Mecca with his eyes still closed. The girl is dumbfounded.

"So here we are on the final pilgrimage!" The Priest declares.

There are incessant tears pouring out of Bhaijan's closed eyes as if he is already seeing what stands in front of him.

"What is this place? And how come we have arrived in a deserted city out of nowhere?" The girl is amazed but not afraid.

"This is Mecca, the most important pilgrimage place for fellow Muslims. It is our Banaras, our Jerusalem.

Paigamber Mohammad, peace be upon his highness, is in his eternal sleep here," the Priest explains. "No Muslim is complete without visiting Mecca and above all, there is nothing left for a true Muslim to desire for, after visiting Mecca. He is beyond the bounding of this mortal world."

"So, was this the final goal of Bhaijan? Is this where he was aspiring to be before dying?" Wonders the girl.

"Yes, this was his last wish and that's why he was working with me in Banaras, to collect enough money to travel to Mecca," the Priest answers. "And that's the only reason he was furious when he heard that I had used all of the money to get you out of the brothel."

"Are we dreaming collectively?" The Girl is still unable to digest the sudden and drastic change of her world.

"Yes, we all are dreaming and we always do. There is nothing new about that. Our life is nothing but a dream. However, here in Mecca we are in the reality of that dream. You can feel and perceive what is happening here. Colors paint reality to our dreams," the Priest elaborates. "So, cherish them and walk around where the enlightened one strolled once upon a time, and preached the lessons of humanity, kindness and explained the unexplainable to his disciples."

The Priest puts on a skullcap and gets off the boat, which is stuck in the sand and looks like a modern-day Noah's Ark.

———————————— ✦ ✦ ✦ ✦ ✦ ✦ ————————————

Azaan for the last Namaaz of the day is being called from the minaret of the Grand Mosque; people clad in white robs are walking in large groups towards the main entrance. Bhaijan is following the Priest, and the girl is behind Bhaijan. She is the only girl approaching the gate from this entrance.

Bhaijan leads thousands of faithful worshippers for the elaborated Namaaz and Sermon. The girl doesn't not understand the message except she always thinks about Bhaijan while repeating the hopeful wish in 'Amen' along with the others.

The prayer meeting disperses as soon as the final sermon is completed. Bhaijan and the Priest are greeting others by hugging them. There are free food stalls outside of the mosque. The faithful are distributing Alms to the poor and rich alike. There is no distinction, no class amongst the pilgrims. Bhaijan and the Priest graciously accept some of the food and head straight back to the boat, the girl follows them.

"I am blessed today; the goal of my mortal life is about to be achieved and you are going to be instrumental in its efforts. You have been the icon for me since the final journey began," Bhaijan speaks while kissing the girl's feet.

"It was such a wonderful feeling to hear the sermon from you Bhaijan. I am amazed, not only at your speech, but also at your sheer commitment that forced nature to pull out a desert right in the middle of the ocean. Really, it is our commitment that controls this world, if we can decide and dedicate ourselves to some objective, there is no reason why we won't achieve it. This is a huge lesson for me," the girl chuckles like a baby who has just learnt how easy it is to walk on her two feet.

"Tel me how can I oblige myself in serving you to attain your dream?" She asks Bhaijan, who is about to cry with bursting emotions.

"Do you know, this is the most important place for any person who follows Islam?" Bhaijan asks her.

"Yes, Aghori told me just a while ago."

Bhaijan is a bit surprised but focused on his conversation. "But, do you know why is it the most important place? It doesn't have any statue, it doesn't have object to revere, just one grave. So, what makes it stand apart?"

"I am not sure, but I think Mohammad was the founder of Islam, so that may be the reason for people to follow and come to this place perhaps?"

"Well, yes, Islam was organized and united by the great Paigamber Mohammad, peace be upon him, but there is more to it. This place is the epitome of all sacrifices. Mohammad laid down his life here for the sake of humanity. He sacrificed every bit of his life for the well-being of wandering souls. Abraham sacrificed his son, Ismail, for the purest of love for his Master, the God. There are countless disciples of Mohammad who laid down their lives so that people can learn that what they are doing is not right, and that they should not get entangled in their own conflicts, but they should try to dream for the ultimate goal, they must aspire to be their true self and conquer their egos."

"And this is what the goal of my life is, and this is what I want you also to do," he further adds this with an emotionally heavy heart.

"I am ready," the girl agrees with him without thinking about the sacrifice she has to make.

"I want you to sacrifice your most beloved thing right here, on this holy land," Bhaijan explains his wish.

"And what is my most valuable thing? My life? I think I can do it easily for you, if that's what the goal of your life is," the girl conforms to Bhaijan's point.

"I don't think your own life is the most valuable thing for you. I don't think life is the most important thing for anyone in this world, had that been the case, no one would have ever wasted a single moment of such a precious thing in their life," Bhaijan tries to correct her.

"Then what is to be sacrificed?" The girl is confused.

"Remember the promise you made to your Adrushya Guru – Aghori: that you will follow his order for him to appear in front of you?" Bhaijan clarifies with a smile. "And in return he will give you one power? You got the power and you used it selflessly to help me in achieving my goal of life, now it is the time that I actually achieve my ultimate goal with your real help."

"Wait, this is Shakespeare to me!! Come straight to the point, I don't know, and neither do I want to delve into these philosophical riddles," the girl is confused in her understanding, but her blunt response drives Bhaijan straight to the point.

"You promised that you will put my physical body to rest once your Adrushya Guru appears in front of you, and also, that you will get one power that may help you in reaching your goal," Bhaijan follows the request.

"Oh, yeah, I did say that and that's why I asked for the power first, and I used it on you. I did it with the hope that you may achieve your goal, but certainly not with the intention that I will have to be a killer of my own savior. I was delaying this murder enforced upon me by my own self," the girl is feeling helpless.

"Not everything that we know as a rule and what we see or hear as

199

guidance is right. Who says that if you sacrifice me, it will be a murder enforced upon you? Who am I? What is the purpose of my life? What are you doing in my life? Why did we help each other and came this far?" Bhaijan tries to convince her. "Everything in this world happens for a reason; we just take those things on our ego, and try to connect them with our logical brain and senses to feed our ego. If we stop just at the reason and try to keep ourselves detached from the consequences, then we will never fall in the trap of our ego. Right now, you are failing to contain yourself at the reason.

You should follow what is right. You should conduct your duty in a true spirit and at present, your duty is to let me go, because, I was destined to this point. Nothing will move from here onwards if I do not reach the conclusion of my duty. Moreover, you are nothing but an instrument to finish the job for me. Remember your duty is more important than your rights.

What you will get in return: a path to your own goal. Aghori mentioned this thing many a times; if you keep on serving your duty, you will keep on getting new horizons that will lead you to your goal."

Bhaijan kneels in front of the girl and bows his head. The girl is holding a shiny sword with some words inscribed in Arabic on its flank in her hands. She is shivering with fear, anxiety, a sense of sin, and above all, anger towards herself.

"La-Ilahe-Ill-Allah," Bhaijan is chanting.

Slowly clouds begin to gather above in the sky. Some people are gathering around the scene. A few of them are curious to see a boat in the desert. Most of them are much more inclined to witness a human sacrifice by a woman. Some men in veils are dissuading the girl not to sacrifice a man; others are slowly raising their voice to finish the job as soon as possible. There is one thing common in the crowd, each and every person looks like a close sibling of the girl.

"Remember, this is the last battle you need to conquer in order to win the war against your ego. There is only one way from here and that goes straight to your destination. What is your destiny? That will be decided by the action you take in the next couple of moments. You still don't know your goal; you have just been wandering to know that. What you are after is nothing but an infinite road," Aghori whispers in her ear. He is standing behind her with his hands on her shoulders.

The sword rises in the air along with rising chants of 'La-Ilahe-Ill-Allah' from Bhaijan as well as the crowd.

The girl's eyes are squeezed shut, and tears are incessantly flowing from them. Her hands are shaking while raising the sword and her jaw is crushingly clenched. Her face is contorted by the agony of what she is just about to do.

"Drop it down! You don't have to think too much. I am here as always, guiding you to do what is required to be done!"

The sword comes down with force, hits one soft object, and then there is complete silence all around. The girl's is still keeping her eyes shut from the fear of the unknown.

A Mullah is calling the azan from a distance for the faithful ones.

The girl slowly drops to the ground; her head is buried between her knees. The sword is slowly slipping out of her hands. The hot air of the desert is rapidly converting to a cool evening breeze.

--- NIRVIKALPA SAMADHI ---
(THE DISSOLUTION)

A splash of cold-water wakes up the girl.

She is still sitting in the same posture as she has been in since she dropped on her knees. She has the sword loosely held in her hands, the Arabic inscription on its blade is shining in the sunlight. The boat is back in the middle of the Indian Ocean now.

She doesn't have any sense of time and she doesn't care about it either. She remains motionless, just breathing in the salty air and thinking about all that has happened in last couple of days. How her life has turned upside-down in the last couple of years.

She can still see the cottage in the Pennsylvanian woods, where it all started. She can still feel the pain of being raped by her own brother, but this time she is just a witness of the brutality; she has the pain but not the anger. There is an action but no reaction from the opposite side.

Once again, she finds herself in the awe of an elderly person in Iran. She knows what she had done with him at first, but the knowledge is that of a fact not of arrogance.

She can still feel the niggling in her nipples from when Aghori tried to breastfeed himself, but she has a sense of motherhood rather than that of a sexual desire.

She can see the ghost standing in front of her with a burning stare but she doesn't have the fear of death anymore. This is the horizon of a new beginning for herself.

She can still see the blue stone in her hand, which she could have used to get anything in this world, including immortality. However, she doesn't have any desires anymore.

She can still smell Bhaijan's blood on the sword but she has no more selfish enchantment for him to be with her always.

She has conquered Anger, Lust, Pride, Enchantment, Greed, and Fear. She is now one with no desire or ego left in her body.

"Now, why should I live?" She asks herself. "If I don't have any desires, if I don't have any ego, if I don't have any duties, then why should I even breathe? I don't think I want to kill my brother anymore, that's behind my goal, but what should be my purpose now?"

"To give, whatever you have; give it to the neediest ones." An unknown voice speaks behind her.

"Who is that?" The girl turns with amazement. The voice is very similar to that of her own.

"I am your Guru. In fact, now you're true-self."

"But that used to be Aghori," the girl counters the reply.

"It is just a matter of voice. It can be anything in this world as your Guru. Now when you have attained such a highest form of purity, you don't need a mirror to look at yourself. You have become light unto yourself. You can see yourself in the infinite of universe," the voice further explains. "Anyway, what does it matter to go into the logic of whom, what and how? Just think about why."

"Ok, so what do you mean by 'to give'?" The girl takes the discussion to her original question.

"You know all the events that happened in your life up till now can be summarized in very simple statement; and that is – Goal of our life is ours, but our life is not for us. It exists to serve the travelers. The moment we achieve our goal, we become one with the supreme soul; we become omnipresent. Either we dissolve in the infinite or we become guides to serve the seekers of ultimate truth. You have attained the highest form of purity to become a guide. So, now lead the journeymen, and help them in attaining their goal." The voice details out the next role for her in this world. "Even an animal's life is meant to be of service to others. They serve us in all forms; they give us comfort as companions, or they may become food for the starving ones so that people can walk towards their goal. Look at your Breach. But, alas! The misguided so-called intelligentsia claim, 'it's my life'."

"So, I still have the same question, what should I do to become a Guide now?" The girl asks the same question.

"You do what you are destined to do without bringing any sense of defeat, ego, pride or sorrow in your mind. Flow like river Ganga, and even if you are in the ocean, you will maintain your identity until your goal is achieved."

"Wait for the right disciple. The boat will lead you to him. Help him to continue on his journey without any prejudice."

"OK, thanks, I will do." The girl replies and stands up to look at the horizon.

The sky suddenly turns dark. There is a huge hurricane rising in front of her eyes, but she has weathered many such storms, and is now quite prepared to weather this one as well.

"Please help me to break this prison and liberate myself!" Someone is shouting from the storm...

--- THE JOURNEY BEGINS ---